# EARL OF HALSBURG

## MAKE MINE AN EARL SERIES
### BOOK 4

# ANNA ST CLAIRE
USA TODAY BESTSELLING AUTHOR

*Dedicated to those who rescue dogs and cats.*
*May they experience the pure love, devotion, and pure selflessness these animals give to their families.*

*The best heroes have fur and four legs.*

*Love is the master key
which opens the gates to happiness.*

~ Oliver Wendell Holmes, Sr.

# CHAPTER 1

*D*isgusted, Alan Hardin, the third Earl of Halsburg, stared at the note he had just received in the morning post. It was the second time in as many weeks he had received one—but this one elevated his concern. "Travers," he called out, stopping the bespeckled, lanky butler as he passed the door to his study.

"Do you recall who left the correspondence with no return name or address?" Alan asked.

"No, my lord. I found it on the top step this morning—only an hour ago."

"I see. That will be all," he said, dismissing the butler, before a thought hit him. "Wait," he said before Travers could take a step.

The butler turned back to face him. "Yes, my lord?"

"Did my uncle ever inquire about a note such as this, one that arrived so . . . mysteriously?" Hardin asked. This was the second such note Alan had received in the past month—and in the year he had been an earl, he realized. The first note he had kept but didn't take seriously. But a second meant someone was determined to make a point. *But what point?* This note bothered him, and he planned to find out who had sent it.

The butler stood for a long moment, perceptibly giving serious thought to the question. "Now that you inquire, my lord, I recall there was a time such a note arrived. It was a month before the carriage accident. I know that because we had a footman to start that day, and I had been training him when he stopped me. He asked me if I knew who had left it, much as you have. It, too, was delivered before sunrise. I believe he mentioned his plans to contact the magistrate, but I cannot be sure. However, he asked me at the time to have his solicitor come to see him."

His uncle's death had been an accident. The magistrate said the horses had been spooked and, as a result, the carriage flipped, trapping his uncle beneath the wreckage. "Did the magistrate ask you questions after his death?" Alan asked.

"No, my lord. The only time he visited was to alert us of the accident and the earl's demise," the butler returned, his response coming slower and more introspective than it had been.

The management of the estate had been thrust at him, so Alan ran things much as his uncle had run things, including his solicitor, so he used the same firm as his uncle had done, including using the same legal firm. "Send word to my solicitor that I wish to see him," Alan said, staring at the note. "Let me know when he plans to come. Also, have the room my mother enjoys using prepared. She plans to be here this week."

"On that, my lord. Her ladyship sent word yesterday evening from the coaching inn that she expected to arrive later today. Her note indicated only that she would want a . . . hot bath upon arrival."

*Had sweat appeared on Traver's upper lip at the mention of his mother?* Hardin bit the inside of his cheek to keep from smiling. His mother was certainly a force of nature. While she treated his servants as her own, she maintained civility; therefore, he felt no reason to intercede. She didn't interfere with his life, and he gave her free rein when she visited. "I trust you to oversee her arrival and see to whatever she requires." His uncle had rarely entertained, and Alan allowed the servants to go about their business, rarely causing a ripple in their day. But when his mother visited, all that changed. The townhouse hummed with activity.

"Yes, my lord." The man turned to leave, but turned back. "I alerted the housekeeper and sent the cook to the market this morning to select the special foods your mother prefers."

"Thank you, Travers," Alan said, glancing once again at the note before looking up. Mrs. Nimble and Mrs. Canary knew exactly what his mother required. "That is all." He would find out what they had discussed. His experience as a spy for the Crown told him this was too coincidental and worth investigating. A niggling concern surfaced with the timing of his mother's visit, but he pushed it away.

"Yes, my lord," Travers said.

"I want the outside of our house watched round the clock. Assign a footman to watch the front of the house. Hire two more if you need the staff. Not only do I want a report on whom you plan to hire before you offer the position, but I wish to meet them as well. Make sure you investigate their background thoroughly. This is the second such note that has been delivered. I want to know how and who is delivering them—and the need for security became heightened with this second one."

The butler brightened, perhaps glad to have something to do other than please Alan's mother. "Yes, my lord. I will see to it."

"I look forward to seeing your selections. It needs to be done immediately, so make it your priority," Alan added.

When his butler left, he reached into the desk drawer and withdrew the first note he had received only weeks earlier, placing it side-by-side with the latest one, comparing them. The handwriting appeared identical, but he doubted that helped. Both letters were hand-printed in what appeared to be an attempt to conceal the sender's identity. The message on this second note was as direct as the first:

*You should not be the earl...*

The first note had been more circumspect, and while he had not discarded it, he had not felt alarmed by it. This second one, however, drew alarm.

*Fraud! Why did you inherit?*

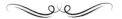

ALAN WAS NOT a happy man as he mounted the granite steps of 276 Bedford Street to meet his friends. One look in his eyes foretold his black mood. He had accepted the earldom but had not been pleased. A year ago, life had seemed so orderly. He had returned from a Crown assignment, only to be told his uncle had died suddenly and that he had inherited an earldom—something he had never coveted. Additionally, he became the guardian of his uncle's best friend's daughters. Not something he expected or enjoyed. Up to now, he had signed off on anything his solicitor recommended. The one meeting he had held with the girls' stepmother, Baroness Rollins, had not gone well, forcing him to remind her of his position. She had a reputation as a greedy woman and an unpleasant one at that. He planned to keep their dealings short and had asked his solicitor to pay the modiste and other vendors directly on the daughters' behalf, instead of giving it to Lady Rollins.

Christmastide would be upon them soon, and he was glad he had agreed to his mother's London visit. He needed to reconnect with his wards and thought his mother would enjoy helping with the two young ladies. The eldest was twenty and the other fourteen; at twenty-five, his age gave him a decided disadvantage, at least with the eldest. She was as attractive a woman as he had ever seen. An oval face framed by thick, russet-colored hair and green eyes. *Or were they hazel?* He closed his eyes, determined to shut her out of his mind. After the first and only time he had met her, her image had haunted his dreams.

He would be her guardian for less than six months. *Surely, I can maintain my priorities and be the guardian she requires.* In that vein, a recent bill from a local modiste left him with questions about the baroness and his charges. It seemed the young ladies might get *short-shifted*. He needed to think creatively about this guardianship and felt his mother's presence might provide the answer.

His solicitor's visit earlier in the day had been arduous. Mr. Penman confirmed his uncle's death had been listed as an accident, and he confirmed his uncle had contacted him about a similar note a few weeks before his death. Since the circumstances of the carriage accident looked cut and dry, no investigation had ensued. But after today's note, and Alan's discovery his uncle had also received a similar one, Alan wondered if it had been an accident. Since no one had investigated Uncle Edward's death, evidence that might have proven something to the contrary might prove difficult to uncover. Alan had the power and resources to investigate, and as a trained solicitor himself, he recognized slapdash work by investigators. Beyond annoyed, he wondered if he had inherited not only an earldom but also a target on his back.

As if that wasn't enough, his solicitor had complained about the welfare of his wards, two daughters of the closest friend of his uncle, who had died six months before his uncle—Miss Elizabeth Rollins and Miss Penny Rollins. This only added to his suspicion that things were not going as he had hoped. The report about his wards had been unexpected, but in this, he planned to garner his mother's help. Perhaps it would distract her from her unrelenting reminder that he must marry and secure the future of the earldom. Alan hoped her focus on the girls might give his household a much-needed break from her scrutiny.

The large, nondescript townhouse blended with those around it. Except for its red door marked with a *W*, it looked no different. Alan knocked at the door as he fingered the small gold 'W' insignia on the pin anchoring his neckcloth. It was a modest emblem, but every member was required to wear his when in attendance. He had been presented with the pin a year ago, following his induction into the club.

While the club was not in the most fashionable district, it

compared favorably with White's, but only with the richness of its interiors. The walls were papered in either deep burgundy or hunter-green tones throughout, and the lighting was low. Only the most masculine furniture—rich leathers, dark wood grains—appointed the club's public rooms. The membership used the club as both a meeting place and a den of pleasures—depending on desire or need. Alan resisted the seedier aspects of the club but found it an excellent place to relax and meet with friends.

"Lord Halsburg, welcome,"

"Thank you, Stewart. Two friends plan to join me for a drink. I'm sure you recall Lord Shefford."

"I do. He was a member a few years past."

"Yes, Shefford will have his brother, Mr. Jonathan Nelson, with him. Nelson's the proprietor of the new fencing club, *En Garde.*

"I understand, my lord." The older man's lip twitched, but he maintained his haughty demeanor. "Your friends await you in the club room—they are seated near the fireplace."

Halsburg quirked his brow. "Thank you, Stewart." He felt his mood lifting, despite the feeling the cards had been stacked against him. "Have someone bring me a brandy."

"Yes, my lord. Right away."

"Shefford, Nelson," he said, shaking their hands before taking the empty leather chair beside them. "I'm glad to see the two of you and could use some advice."

"My lord, your brandy," a footman said, approaching from behind and placing Alan's brandy on the small table beside his chair.

"If you want to ask about marriage, I highly recommend it," quipped his best friend, Colin Nelson, the Earl of Shefford. "I just need to find someone to tempt my brother here into settling down."

"I'm tremendously happy for you and your lovely countess. However, marriage-minded mothers are one thing I have not enjoyed since attaining the earldom. While I have no immediate aversion to marriage, I find the cloying debutantes and their mothers tiresome and avoid them at all costs," Alan said, chuckling.

"Colin's about to wear us all down with his perpetual cheer these days," said his brother, Jonathan Nelson with a laugh. "I can, however, attest it hasn't taken the edge off his fencing. My customers ask to fence with Colin, perhaps because of his newly gained master's status.

"Please, don't . . . Jonathan," Colin said, swirling his drink and turning a slight shade of pink. "It was a requirement for opening the club—we needed two masters."

"That makes good sense. I've heard good things about the club. How's it been doing?" Alan asked. The brothers had opened the fencing club to honor their father's influence in their lives. Both men were considered fencing masters, a title only given to the most accomplished. "If you'd like to expand, I would be an interested investor. *En Garde* may do for fencing enthusiasts what Jackson's has for pugilists."

"That's a nice offer and we will keep it in mind. The club has been a tremendous undertaking, but Jonathan operates it carefully, which has been tremendously beneficial for everyone," Shefford replied.

"It's been in great demand among the *ton*," Jonathan agreed.

"Our fencing training was helpful during the war. Has that affected admission applications?" Alan asked.

"Yes, we've seen a lot of interest," Shefford said.

"And I hope it stays that way," Nelson bantered.

"I'm glad our venture has been successful. But that isn't why you asked to meet," Shefford said.

"I'm in earnest about becoming a silent partner, so if you decide to pursue expansion, speak with me." Alan's face became pensive. "You are right, though. I need your advice. I've gotten two notes—strange ones questioning my legitimacy as heir."

"How could that be? Your father—your uncle's only brother—predeceased him, and your uncle was without issue," Shefford put in.

"Exactly. And if that wasn't strange enough, I discovered this morning my uncle had received a similar note—delivered with no one seeing who left it—shortly before the accident. I can only guess what they wrote but, without finding it, I have no way to know. It seems coincidental," he said, withdrawing the notes from his pocket and passing them to his friends, "but pertinent."

Shefford read the notes and quietly passed them to his brother.

Jonathan looked up after the second note. "Same person wrote it. It certainly would be helpful to have the note your uncle received. Have you sorted through the office to see if it's still there?"

"I hadn't thought of that," Alan admitted. He'd begin looking immediately. Perhaps Travers would remember if his uncle had mentioned anything.

"If your uncle received something similar and died in a coaching accident that wasn't investigated . . ." Shefford began. "You may have a target on your back."

"My thoughts exactly," Alan said.

"It somewhat takes the shine off of being elevated to the peerage," Shefford said.

"Yes. It does. While I don't see how that can be changed, I don't plan to have my life snuffed out over primogeniture. I plan to find whoever is sending the threatening notes to me," Alan said.

"What can we do to assist?" Shefford asked.

"You've heard me out and don't feel I'm off track. That's tremendous support. I sent a note to the palace before I left the house, requesting an audience with the king's agent. My father died, and outside of my younger brother and myself, there were no other males. But I'm wondering about the transition *before* my uncle's inheritance and need to investigate. If someone has a question, that might be where we find them," Alan conjectured.

"The king's agent's name is Ruben—*Mr. John Ruben*," Nelson said. "I contact him frequently with applicants at our school when there are questions. The last thing I want is for our school to gain notoriety for a bad actor who uses the skills we teach them dissolutely. "I'll put Ruben in contact with you."

# CHAPTER 2

"Miss Elizabeth, you are being summoned," her abigail said, gently tapping her charge on the shoulder. "You have little time to dress."

Miss Elizabeth Rollins had finally found sleep, trying to make up for the nightmare that had woken her up and stolen most of her sleep. She reached over and pulled the extra pillow over the back of her head—a poor attempt to deny her abigail's request that she leave her warm bed. She hated anything that required her to spend time with her stepmother. *What new cruelty does the woman have planned for me today?*

Since Papa's death, the Widow Rollins turned each day into a fresh assault on Elizabeth's way of life; little by little, something was taken away. In the week following the reading of her father's will, she was *temporarily* removed from the room she had spent all her life in and placed in a smaller guest room further down the hallway. They had refitted her larger bedroom as a guest room for her stepmother's sister, Louisa, who had visited. She had been informed her aunt was a sleepwalker and needed to be closer to her older sister. The woman had stayed two months and, as far as Elizabeth knew, never walked in her sleep while she was there. And they still had not put the rooms back to rights.

Two weeks ago, her stepmother's attention had turned to Elizabeth's wardrobe, when she had canceled Elizabeth's seasonal trip to the modiste. *"Your father died and did not leave enough for us to buy you new clothes this Season, and I need new clothes. I cannot afford to be seen in yesterday's fashions. But I have observed Jane is good with the needle and will repair and adjust your dresses. Of course, you will be permitted new half-boots, gloves, incidentals, and of course, a new pelisse,"* Lady Rollins had said, as they approached the coach for the trip to town.

Christmastide was nearly upon them. Needlepoint was not her strong suit and there was little she could make for her sister. Elizabeth had counted on the shopping trip. Her younger sister, Penny, deserved a decent Christmas and Elizabeth would make sure she received one. She had carefully placed her saved pin money in a carved-out area of a book and placed it inconspicuously on her small bookshelf. It was reminiscent of a book her father had shown her from his library. Papa had been a rich man—far wealthier than many of his peers. *What had happened to his money? Surely, things were not as dire as her stepmother made them out to be.*

"Is Penny awake?" Elizabeth asked in muffled tones from beneath the pillow.

"Yes, Miss Penny is with her governess. I heard . . ." Jane started but stopped.

Her maid sounded distressed. *"What . . . what did you hear, Jane?* Please tell me, especially if it involves my sister."

"Cook told me the governess has been dismissed, effective in one week."

"But why?" Elizabeth asked, sitting and running her hand through her hair. "Penny loves her governess. Why would Delores sack Miss Mary?"

"I'm sorry, miss. 'Tis all Cook knew," Jane said. "But perhaps she will tell you. She is most insistent that you join her in the drawing room. I saw . . . uh . . . her son arrived earlier."

Elizabeth pulled the pillow over her head more tightly as a

shudder wound its way through her. Daniel Chadwick was a lecher. He would chase her around the house and try to touch her—something she never told a soul, instinctively fearing her stepmother. Her son was rude and mean. Elizabeth watched her pets closely and kept them away from Daniel, always recalling when the barn cat was found drowned near the pond. She had been horrified, intuitively knowing it was him, but having no evidence. Until he left home, she had not taken another as a pet, fearing what Daniel would do to it. Her horse, Sable, was dear to her, and she rode her as often as she could. She would make sure the ostler knew Daniel was back. Joe knew the boy was capable of mean things. He had helped her bury the mother cat and the kittens, both of them crying. Elizabeth had never seen a man cry before that, and it made her appreciate Joe more.

"Papa banned him after he . . ." Elizabeth stopped in mid-sentence, reminded of a stern lecture she once received from her father about discussing family affairs with the staff, *even if that was Jane—who practically grew up alongside her as a sister.* It had been Joe's daughter Daniel had ravished. Joe kept it quiet, except for her father and her. Joe had become her protector, making sure Elizabeth knew to never be alone with Daniel. He always requested Ross or one of the other footmen ride behind Elizabeth. *"Not that the staff won't know,"* Papa had explained. *"Rather, it is poor form to engage in such discussion."*

Her father had lost his heart the day Mama died. It hadn't helped that her younger sister was the image of her mother, blonde with blue eyes. Elizabeth looked like her father. Papa had become desolate, different, and buried himself in his business dealings—and for a short time, couldn't bring himself to hold Penny. Gradually, after much coaxing from his friends, he reemerged, finding joy in his daughters, and resurfacing into Society—supposedly to find a mother for his girls.

Delores was a young widow who had got her hooks in her father quickly. Elizabeth saw her as everything her mother had not been in temperament—moody, vain, and jealous. Once they married and he moved her into the house, things changed . . . subtlety, at first. It started with Mama's gardens, which were changed. Delores uprooted her beloved roses and replaced them with boxwoods and other shrubs. It seemed to Elizabeth the woman was trying to erase everything to do with her mother's existence. For right now, however, Elizabeth needed to survive. "Help me prepare for the harridan," she whispered to her maid.

Jane nodded. "Then let's decide on what to wear," her maid said thoughtfully. "I've taken stock of your clothes and there are several dresses, including your favorite rose satin, that needed no repair. And unless the styles have changed tremendously, you should be fine for social occasions," Jane said.

"I'll wear my dark blue day dress. It's comfortable," Elizabeth replied.

"Blimey! One of these days, the woman will figure you out," Jane said, smiling.

Blue had been her mother's favorite color, and Delores knew that. Wearing blue had become Elizabeth's way of poking the bear. Delores' irritation was palpable, but she was not an intelligent woman and Elizabeth's subtle retaliation never dawned on her.

Thirty minutes later, Elizabeth stood in front of the door to the drawing room. Taking a deep breath, she pushed the door open and entered. Her stepmother, Delores, sat with her back at the door, reading a paper. Her son peered up from his plate, seated in the seat her father had always occupied at the other end, and did not stand when she entered. Typical of his manners . . . *lacking*, Elizabeth thought.

"Ah, Elizabeth. So nice to see you again," her son finally said from his seat. Once he had taken another drink from his cup, he put down his paper and stood, walking to the sideboard for a second helping of eggs and rashers before retaking his seat, wasting no regard on Elizabeth.

"Daniel," the baroness said with a tight smile, pulling tightly on her face. "Perhaps you can assist Elizabeth with her breakfast."

*Which made Elizabeth wonder what her stepmother had in mind for today.*

"Yes, Mother," Daniel said, putting down his utensils and standing. "Miss Elizabeth." He pulled out the chair nearest his own for her.

"I'll take my usual seat, but thank you," Elizabeth said, choosing the chair in front of the sidebar, placing her as far as possible from the loathsome man. A shudder of foreboding shook her. From the corner of her eye, Elizabeth caught her stepmother's eyes narrowed in her direction, but when Elizabeth glanced up, the woman quickly schooled her face.

"Darling Elizabeth, Daniel has moved back home," her stepmother said pointedly. "He requires a larger room, as did my poor sister. It is my hope you will not object to his use of your former room."

Biting her bottom lip to avoid saying what she wanted to say, which would most certainly lead to more trouble, Elizabeth choked back her retort. "No, Stepmother. I do not mind. I'm quite comfortable in my new room."

Her stepmother's brows lifted in surprise. "Then, it is settled," the baroness said, taking a bite of her toast. "I almost forgot. There is one more thing I should mention," she said acerbically as she sipped her tea. "I dismissed Miss Mary."

"But . . . but why? Penny loved her. And she was doing so well." Elizabeth struggled to keep her temper in check.

"I found the woman lacking. And while I feel you would be a more suitable person to see to your sister's education, Daniel pointed out the unsuitability of that arrangement." She smiled in her son's direction, almost reverently.

Elizabeth glanced from the mother to the son and would have sworn each smirked at the other. *My birthday cannot come soon enough,* she thought, thankful she had saved most of her pin money for the two years before her father's death. Otherwise, she could not leave the house. She would not allow this to happen. "Did Lord Halsburg approve of the dismissal?" she asked in a voice devoid of emotion. Lord Halsburg, as her father's best friend's nephew, had been named the guardian of both her and her sister until they came of age, after his uncle died.

The baroness tossed her napkin down and stood. "How dare you

question me! I run this household. Not Lord Halsburg. I can dismiss . .
."

"A servant Lord Halsburg hired and pays?" Elizabeth cut in, firmly. Pride stiffened her backbone. She would show no fear to her stepmother.

From the corner of her eye, Elizabeth noted a strange, silent communication between mother and son. A subtle shake of her son's head had her stepmother retaking her seat. Her countenance changed. "Of course, you are right, and I had forgotten that. Excuse my outburst. The stress of your father's absence has worn my patience quite thin. So many things have changed, and I miss him so." She took a steadying breath. "Dear Daniel pointed out my misstep, and I rehired the woman, of course."

"Thank you, Stepmother," Elizabeth said, cautiously exercising a tried-and-true response she had learned over the years worked on the woman. The woman's vanity needed constant mollifying, and Elizabeth had learned long ago a small amount of contrition was a powerful tool.

The door opened, and Walters stepped inside. "Lady Rollins, Miss Rollins," the butler said. "Lord Halsburg has sent his footman with an invitation. He awaits your response," the butler said, offering the salver with the invitation in its center.

Elizabeth didn't miss Walters' omission of her son in his greeting. But Walters had been here for ages and if Delores dismissed him, the rest of the staff would likely follow him.

Her stepmother snatched it and opened it. Recalling how her stepmother had torn up a previous invitation from the Halsburg residence after the reading of the will, Elizabeth watched the side of her stepmother's mouth twitch in anger. Placing the vellum on the table, the baroness scowled at Elizabeth. "It seems they have invited us to Earl Halsburg's residence for dinner. They have included your sister," she said haughtily. "Certainly, they are unaware Daniel has temporarily moved home. Walters, give us a few minutes."

"Yes, Lady Rollins," the older man said, stepping outside the door.

Elizabeth glimpsed her stepbrother from beneath her lashes and didn't miss the pull of his mouth in a grimace at his mother's revelation he had moved back home. But the man restrained from comment. Yet, his drinking and gambling were no secret and had been a constant source of conflict between her stepparent and her father. Papa had not only banned her stepbrother from the house, but shortly before he had died, Elizabeth had overheard a heated discussion between her father and Daniel as she passed her father's study. Her father had told Daniel he would no longer pay his debts, meaning Daniel would have to live on an allowance. The amount he gave Daniel was not much bigger than that of her own monthly pin money. Elizabeth had bitten the back of her hand to keep from making noise as she tip-toed past the door of the study to the stairwell and ducked into her departed mother's parlor—the only place that was still decorated in the colors her mother had chosen.

"I was unaware you had moved home permanently. I thought this was a surprise visit, Daniel," Elizabeth said carefully. Turning to her stepmother, she said, "When is the dinner?"

"It's in two days," she bit off, apparently attempting to maintain a calm demeanor. "I have changed my mind and have made an appointment with the modiste today. I will see what she has that is ready-made and can be adjusted to your size. We will find somewhere else to trim expenses. Your pelisse is also ready, so I will bring that home as well. Perhaps while there, we will find something to match it."

"Thank you, Stepmother," Elizabeth managed, recalling the last time her stepmother selected a dress for her. "But coincidentally, Jane pointed out the deep rose satin dress this morning. It should need little to no alteration."

"Excellent. Then, it is settled. I will send word back to Lord Halsburg."

# CHAPTER 3

THE NEXT DAY

"Time to awaken, my lord," Everly said, opening the heavy green drapes and pulling them to one side of the wall. "Your mother just arrived, and the house is abuzz with activity. She is asking to see you in the drawing room so you may break your fast together."

"Did she say what delayed her arrival?" Alan asked sleepily, squinting at the bright light streaming into his room.

"No, my lord. But she seems to have a burr under her saddle if you catch my meaning. Something unexpected may have delayed her," Everly said carefully, as he laid out the earl's clothing. "Your bath is drawn, and I will return to assist in a little while."

He opened his mouth to correct the overstep of his valet but bit his tongue. "Thank you, Everly. I shall require a shave, so I'll make quick work of the bath." Their relationship had allowed verbal frankness on the battlefield. Sometimes, his candor had helped. They had bonded together on the frontline, and in that regard, they were brothers in arms.

"Yes, my lord. I will retrieve your boots while you bathe and can shave you when I return."

"That gives me time to wake up," Alan said, dragging himself from the warmth of the bed and wrapping his top sheet around his lower torso. "I stayed at the club a little longer last night. But it was good to see Shefford and Nelson."

"Two of my favorites, my lord," Everly said, walking towards the door before stopping at the door. "That reminds me. You were gone when James returned from the Rollins' house. But the baroness agreed to come to dinner tomorrow."

"Excellent," Alan said. "I wish to see both young ladies for myself."

"Yes, my lord."

Penman told him the baroness was diverting funds intended for his wards. He shook his head in disbelief. *The young ladies and my mother's presence should subdue my temper.* "Have Mrs. Canary consult with my mother on the menu."

"To be sure, the baroness will question her dubious actions towards your wards before the last course of dinner is served," the valet said, dipping his head before departing the room.

"That is my hope," Alan muttered, stepping into the copper tub of steaming water.

Once dressed, Alan hurried to the drawing room. His stomach rumbled at the familiar smells. "Hello, Mother," he said, walking into the room and taking his seat opposite his mother. "It's wonderful to see you this sunny winter morning."

"You've nailed the weather, son." His mother placed her fork down. "But I suspect there's an additional meaning behind those cheery words."

"Can't a son be pleased to see his mother?" Alan asked, with his back to his mother while he added rashers and toast to his plate.

Taking his seat, Alan shook out his napkin before placing it on his lap.

"I would hope so, but this time you sound too pleased," she said, amused. "Out with it."

Alan struggled to bite back his smile. "I have a favor to ask you, Mother."

"I knew it!" she said, smugly taking a bite of her eggs. "How can I help?"

Taking a sip of his coffee, Alan gave a moment to think about his approach. Direct was usually the best way with his mother. It would help him in a couple of ways if his mother would help with his wards. She was just the right foil for the baroness, too. "I need you to take the lead in helping me with my two wards. According to my solicitor, Mr. Penman—who, as you recall, was also Uncle Edward's solicitor—Lady Rollins is diverting my efforts to care for the two Rollins ladies and lining her pockets with whatever money I'm turning loose for their care."

"How so? You're certain he didn't misunderstand her intentions?"

"There's little chance of that, Mother. Penman spoke with the modiste, and all the outfits charged to me were for Lady Rollins. The girls got no new dresses. She allowed them a few things, like a pair of half-boots and a new coat, but no new dresses. I have purposely invited the baroness, Miss Elizabeth Rollins, and her sister Penny for dinner tomorrow."

"And she accepted," his mother said, astonished. "Surely she doesn't expect to get away with denying the proper upkeep for the girls!"

"I believe she does. And that is why I need your help. I find my attention must be elsewhere, but I cannot allow this woman to take advantage of these girls. Miss Elizabeth Rollins missed the last two Seasons—possibly because of her father's death. But I must ensure that Miss Rollins takes part in the next Season, and her sister must have a proper young lady's education and have everything she needs. I need someone to help these young women."

"I have never had a daughter and would love to see to the young Rollins girls. And I assure you, they will gain the advantage of having a very thoughtful and caring guardian—you—who is acting in their best interest. When was the last time you spoke with them?"

Alan glanced away before looking his parent in the eye. "It's been almost a year. That may be why she thinks she can ignore my requests. So, I bear some responsibility."

"*Well, no more!* I will make sure she takes nary a farthing that belongs to those lovely girls," the countess said.

"Thank you, Mother. That takes an enormous weight off my shoulders. It will make my job as guardian more effective in this case," Alan said.

"You mentioned dinner. I take it, she will come under protest," his mother supposed.

"I sent James to relay my invitation, and she accepted, but he said he heard loud voices from inside the drawing room. And she has taken her son, Daniel, back into the home," Alan added.

"The son that the solicitor told us Lord Rollins had banned for illicit behavior toward the upstairs maid?" she said in astonishment.

"Yes. According to Penman, Lord Rollins had banned Daniel Chadwick from the estate. Shortly before his death, Rollins had withdrawn his support for his stepson's gambling and drinking. Chadwick had been running up debts and asking his stepfather to pay. But he stopped that. There was more, but you get the idea. And the boy is back at home, so he will accompany the baroness to dinner tomorrow evening."

The sparkle in his mother's eyes was all the answer he needed. Perhaps this would provide the countess with the diversion she needed.

A knock preceded Traver's entrance. "My lord, you have a guest—Mr. Ruben."

"I have been expecting him. Have him wait in my study." Wiping his mouth with his napkin, Alan stood to leave, then he walked to his mother and kissed her on her head. "Thank you, Mother. I appreciate you so much."

"I will quite enjoy this, son," she said, sipping her tea. "Thank you." The countess picked up her gossip rag and resumed reading it.

He'd have to thank Nelson when he saw him next. Mr. Ruben had arrived much earlier than he had expected. "Thank you for coming, Mr. Ruben," he said, extending his hand to his guest.

A blond man with greying temples and a slight paunch entered the room. "Mr. Nelson and Lord Shefford suggested we meet, my lord. I found myself on this side of London today and thought I would take the chance to stop by to see if we could meet," Ruben said. The shorter man took the seat in front of the earl's desk.

"Would you like some brandy?" Alan asked, setting out two glasses next to the decanter.

"Yes, thank you," Ruben said, accepting a glass.

Alan sipped his brandy and sat back in his chair. "I suppose I should get straight to the point," Alan said. "I believe my uncle could have been murdered, even though his death was considered an accident."

"What makes you believe so, Lord Halsburg?" Ruben asked.

"For one, these letters." Alan reached into his desk drawer and withdrew the two letters and handed them to the man. "Not meaning to confuse you, but I received these."

The man looked up, puzzled.

"Yes, I know what you are thinking, but when I questioned Travers, my butler, about these, he mentioned my uncle had also received one shortly before his death—something his solicitor confirmed. I found that odd, so I did some checking, and it seems that my uncle's death might not have been an accident. Uncle Edward contacted the solicitor about the note he received and asked him to find out if anyone else—or the relative of anyone else—had possibly laid claim on his title. Nothing surfaced. And now, a year after I've inherited, I am receiving the notes." He eyed Ruben, hoping to gauge his thoughts, but the man maintained a very emotionless façade. "What do you think, Ruben?"

The man picked up the notes, read them, and laid them face up on the table. "Someone has you in their sights, my lord."

"That seems to be the consensus." Hearing someone else say what he had also thought sent chills down Alan's spine. "And what do I do about it? Do *you* know of anyone that has openly my coveted title?"

"I do not, my lord. But it is difficult to pick up on those nuanced comments if you are not listening for them," he said, taking a sip of his brandy. "Tell me more about your role as guardian. Often the transition to guardianship can make for a bumpy road, but these things clear up . . . often with no one losing their life over it," he said, chuckling.

Alan ignored the dig. "It's not been smooth sailing, but that is because of Lady Rollins, the widow. She resents my involvement and attempts to thwart me on every move with the girls, this time canceling their modiste appointments. Instead, she bought clothing for herself and had the bill sent to me."

"My, that is blatant," Ruben observed. "And stupid."

"Yes. She is rather shallow. Normally, I would not have checked it, but I have grown suspicious of her, so we contacted the modiste. While the visit was the same day I had arranged for my wards, she canceled the girls' appointments and used them for herself. Of course, when I call her on it—which I intend to do—she will blame it on the modiste." Alan swirled the brandy in his glass contemplatively.

"Wasn't the girls' father, Baron Rollins, wealthy? He was rumored to have more money than many of the peers of the realm. What odd behavior?" Ruben inquired.

"I agree. And with everything else—especially the receipt of these notes—my concerns must be on more important matters. I have asked my mother to assist me with the young ladies, and she has graciously accepted the challenge," Alan said.

Both men chuckled. "I can imagine her ire when she finds she is being managed by another woman—and one who is not intimidated by her position," Ruben said thoughtfully.

"I had not considered that, especially when she married Lord Rollins to achieve her position. Before that, she had . . . traveled outside our circles," Alan added thoughtfully. "Mother can handle herself. And I explained what had been going on."

"I should like to meet your mother one day. I have heard many good things about her. Forgive me. I don't mean to make you uncomfortable."

Ruben's comment caught him by surprise, and despite himself, Alan felt disordered over the comment. The agent, Mr. Ruben, was a handsome man and worked for the king. *Good God! Was he upset because the man was attracted to his mother?* Yet, maybe he could use making a match for his mother as another tactic to divert her attention from finding him a wife. He shook his head. *No.* He could not get comfortable with that, tempting as it might be. But he would pass the message to his mother. "I appreciate that, Ruben. Perhaps another time, she may be in attendance. But I believe she is running errands." His attention drifted to the study door for a second. *Don't make a liar out of me and waltz through my study door, Mother.*

"Yes, well, I apologize if I made you feel awkward," Ruben began. "I find myself lonely these days, that is all. My wife died five years ago. An attractive woman who is my age and shares my interests appeals to me greatly. I noticed Lady Hardin at a function earlier this year, but never gained an introduction."

The man took a healthy drink of brandy, inspiring Alan to take a fortifying drink himself.

"Do you have any other concerns, Halsburg?"

"I do," Alan replied. "Her son has moved into the house. I have it on good authority that he spends a great deal of time in the opium dens, not to mention the gaming houses. I should like to find out what you know about his debts—only because he now lives with his mother, and, of course, my wards." Unexpectedly, Elizabeth Rollins' dimpled face with large green eyes came to mind. He blinked. *Where did that come from? How has she wormed her way back into my mind?*

"You realize you could bring your wards here to live?" Ruben prodded.

*Just what I'd need. I'd never get her off my mind.* "Frankly, I've thought that out of the question . . . at least before my mother came; it would not have been appropriate. I would rather they stay where they are comfortable unless it is necessary to move them. However, I will mention it to Mother."

"I reference it only as an option. Give me a few days to poke around about the son. What is his name?" Ruben asked.

"Daniel Chadwick."

"That sounds strangely familiar," Ruben replied, thoughtfully.

"My solicitor tells me the baron stopped paying for the boy's gambling debts. And they banned him from the family homes for attempting to ravage a housemaid. That had been a discussion between my uncle and his friend. But somehow, he has found his way back . . ." Alan let the sentence die as two other thoughts popped into his head. "No one has been named the baron's successor. Is his barony reverting to the Crown?"

"It *has* reverted to the Crown. No legitimate heir could be found. However, the baron had extremely healthy financial resources and was wealthy outside of the barony," Ruben said. "That includes the townhouse in Mayfair. However, I doubt being turned out by the baron had any effect on his habits."

"I had given thought to that, too. However, it is a direction to look . . . if only as it affects my wards. Would you mind letting me know what you find?" Alan asked.

"Not at all. I suggest you pay close attention to both him and his mother. Do they know how much wealth you are managing for the girls? There was a great deal of wealth there."

"I had not considered that point. But I will ask my solicitor."

"Thank you, Lord Halsburg," Ruben said, draining his glass and standing. He turned serious. "I will investigate these matters for you and revisit any distant relatives that might have felt a slight at your inheriting, especially since the notes appear to question that."

"Good. Thank you for that. Let me hear from you when you have something to tell me," Alan said, walking him to the front door and shaking the man's hand. "It has truly been a pleasure."

"You will hear from me soon," Ruben promised, accepting his hat from Travers, and replacing it on his head.

# CHAPTER 4

THE NEXT DAY

*E*lizabeth rose early and took her horse to Hyde Park, needing to free herself from the tension her stepmother and her son had created. They were up to something. She just knew it. *But what?* She wasn't frightened for herself, but Penny was only fourteen years old. Having Penny so much younger and with no place to go kept Elizabeth under her stepmother's thumb, and she knew it.

She wished with all her heart, she had taken her first two Seasons seriously, but she had never thought she would lose her father and her way of life almost at the same time. She had contemplated finding work as a governess—she could speak French and Italian, play the pianoforte, and paint. Her needlepoint was not her strong suit, but she could make herself do better. Only becoming a governess would mean leaving her sister here. And she couldn't do that. No, her father would expect her to take good care of her sister. And she intended to do just that.

Muffled voices from her father's study down the hall caught her attention as she reentered the house; she was eager to hear but not get caught. Spotting the door to a small room to the left of her father's study, she walked slowly in that direction. The room didn't have a certain name, like a storage closet or pantry. She didn't understand its purpose. The few times she had peeked inside, she had seen stacks of books and things that looked like they belonged in the attic. When she had asked Papa, he had said that his father had had the room built for things he wanted to keep nearby, but not in the study.

It was still early in the morning, and Elizabeth had expected to find everyone still asleep. Holding her breath, careful not to be heard or seen, she edged along the wall. Earlier in the week, Jane had mentioned being approached by her stepmother to keep tabs on Elizabeth, but her maid had refused—at the risk of being turned out. Most of the servants had been with her family since before she was born; however, she would not put it past the baroness to turn one into a snitch.

When Elizabeth tried the doorknob, she was grateful it clicked open, and she quickly slid inside. The muffled tones she had heard earlier were much clearer, and she could hear her stepmother and Daniel.

"I cannot keep giving you money for your habits. You must find someone to marry," the baroness said. "My funds are limited now that George is gone."

"What about *her?*" Daniel asked. "You told me to get closer to Elizabeth."

Elizabeth's body shivered with revulsion.

"Elizabeth and her sister have the bulk of his unentailed properties and wealth, but they are being held in a trust and managed by Halsburg, as their guardian."

"What is it with that man? Why don't you marry him, Mother? Use the same seduction trap you used with the baron."

Elizabeth gasped. *What were they speaking of?*

"Don't be absurd! I am too old to have children now. But George married me in hopes the baby I carried would be a male heir," her stepmother said quietly. She sounded sad.

"Well, why didn't you give him another brat when you lost that one? At least you'd still have the barony . . . until the brat became of age," Daniel said mockingly.

The loud sound of skin smacking skin sounded, almost as if it was next to her.

"Never speak to me like that again, *Daniel*." Her stepmother said angrily. "And never speak of me or my child that way, or I swear, I will turn you out. You are under my roof and will treat me with respect and obey the rules of the house. The opium den is off limits—as are the gambling houses. Find a way to earn money because I cannot support you indefinitely on my measly income, especially with the habits you have developed."

"You suggested I marry Elizabeth. That would solve all my money problems . . ."

"Only if there was a lot of money there and only until your next debt. I've changed my mind. She won't have an endless income," Lady Rollins said, cutting in. "No, you must clean yourself up and find a young heiress that has a title—someone with a large dowry and a rich father that can bail you out of problems. I suggest you court Lady Rose Gunter. This was her second Season, and unless I am mistaken, she failed to gain a marriage proposal."

"What have I to offer her? The baron settled no money on me and didn't think to bestow one of his properties on me. I got nothing," Daniel sneered.

"You have looks and an allowance. Your allowance would have been more had you acted responsibly while he was alive. But no, you had to force yourself on that maid and get thrown out of the house. I told you to keep your hands off the servants," his mother scolded.

"You could have fought to change my allowance, Mother. I have a plan I intend to follow."

Hairs prickled Elizabeth's neck. He sounded so loud, it startled her, briefly thinking he was within inches of her face—even though he stood on the other side of the wall from her.

"Don't sell yourself short. You are intelligent. Do nothing you will regret, son," the baroness said. Her voice had lost the edge moments ago.

"I won't embarrass you, *Mother*," he jeered, exiting the room and slamming the door to the study.

Elizabeth remained still. *What was his plan?* "I have a bad feeling about this," she muttered to herself. A moment later, the door to the study clicked shut and the familiar sound of her stepmother's footsteps moved down the hall toward the parlor. Not wanting to get caught, Elizabeth waited five minutes before emerging. As she walked past the door to the study, Walters rounded the corner and stopped.

The older man gave a knowing look, and in that instant, Elizabeth realized he had seen her. He kept his voice barely above a whisper. "The baroness just closed the door to her parlor, Miss Elizabeth. Hurry upstairs before she steps out." He gave an encouraging nod. "Ross put the horses up. And your stepbrother left the house through the kitchen. I cannot speculate on where he's gone, or for how long, but he was in a rotten temper."

"Thank you, Walters."

"Of course, Miss Elizabeth. I am keeping a pledge I made when your father died to watch over you and your sister, to the best of my ability. Now, go!" he urged.

Humbled by his obvious feeling for her and Penny, Elizabeth hugged him. Then she took off her half-boots and hurried up the stairs, determined to keep the noise to a minimum. Checking the hall and seeing no one, she scurried into her room and shut the door behind her. Elizabeth leaned up against it in relief before a light knock sounded.

She stepped away, just in time for Jane to walk into the room carrying her chocolate and biscuits. "Miss Elizabeth, I thought you might enjoy breaking your fast in your room this morning," Jane said. "I had your bath prepared while you were exercising your horse. You allowed Ross to keep up with you, didn't you?" Jane gave Elizabeth a knowing look. She was known to give the footmen a run to keep up with her, but she had done as she knew her father would have wished this morning and taken it measured and slow. She had needed fresh air away from the smothering persona of her stepmother, and now her son. Her father must be rolling over in his grave, she thought. "Of course. I promised you. Ross rode behind me, but I didn't leave his sight. The last thing I want is to give my wicked stepmother any ammunition to use against my sister or me." An involuntary shudder shook her, as she recalled the conversation she had overheard. "I hope he isn't planning on *me* being part of his . . . plan," she murmured.

"Pardon, miss?"

"I'm sorry, I was speaking a thought out loud," Elizabeth said, horrified she had spoken her thoughts. Thank goodness it was with Jane and not her stepmother. "I'm ready for my bath."

"If you don't mind, miss, I'll tidy up your room while you are bathing. I keep finding things to put away since you changed bedrooms. And I want to assist you in getting ready and making sure we have everything you need for your dinner tonight. I'm afraid that if I leave the room, the baroness finds things for me to do, and it keeps me from assisting you."

"Thank you, Jane. I hope she will leave me alone and let me relax today. The dinner will be stressful, enough. Especially for her." A giggle escaped Elizabeth, as she remembered the baroness's face when she had read the earl's invitation.

"I hope it doesn't sound too impertinent, but I wish I had been a fly on the wall when she read the invitation," Jane said in a loud whisper before both girls dissolved into subdued giggles.

"It was priceless, I'll have to admit," Elizabeth allowed, keeping her voice down, as well. "Jane, you must be careful my stepmother doesn't pick up on your feelings. If she questions your loyalty, she might sack you. And I'm not sure what I would do without you. Promise me."

"I promise, Miss Elizabeth. I will do my best not to draw her ire. But you and Miss Penny should meet the earl and spend time with him if you can. Your father selected his uncle because he's a good man and would care about the welfare of both of you. From what I've heard, this man is good, and he is astute. I heard he was trained as a solicitor before becoming an earl."

"Ha! I won't ask your source. All right . . . I should bathe before the water gets cold. I won't be long." Elizabeth said after Jane helped her with her clothes. She disappeared into a small sitting room she had turned into a dressing room. Grabbing the small bar of jasmine soap before slipping into the warm bath, she sank, allowing the soap to glide over her body. The jasmine scent and warm water made her content to close her eyes and stay there until the water turned ice cold. After what seemed like half an hour, she rose and toweled off, resigned to facing the rest of the day. Somehow, with Daniel's presence, the day had taken on an ominous pallor. After overhearing the conversation earlier, she wondered what was in store for her sister and her. Jane was right. Her guardian was her only hope—a stranger she had only met a few times, but the nephew of the man her father had trusted like a brother. Perhaps she could trust him—*she needed to trust someone.*

Once she was dressed, Elizabeth sat down on the blue and white loveseat she had brought from her bedroom and placed it in front of the fireplace. The heat from the fireplace provided just the warmth she craved. She had recreated this room, determined to make it as comfortable as the one her stepmother had taken from her.

Daniel certainly didn't need her frilly settee. Without asking, she had quietly selected a couple of chairs from another guest room. She had also had Ross and another footman exchange her vanity and other personal items from her old room with the chairs from this one. She realized her stepmother had orchestrated the move just to be mean, but it made her laugh to think of how Daniel must enjoy her sunny yellow room.

This room had been in blue tones, and it was easy enough to transition some of her favorite pieces into it. Smiling, she picked up the book she had been reading. It was a gothic romance—something into which she could immerse herself and escape. Elizabeth settled into the settee and pulled a warm blanket over her stocking feet, as Jane neared the couch. "When Penny is dressed, ask her to join me," Elizabeth said.

"I'll do that, Miss Elizabeth," Jane said as she left the room.

"Mother, I appreciate your willingness to help me," Alan said, leaning down and kissing his mother on the head. "And you look lovely, as usual." His mother never seemed to age. His father had died shortly after his brother had been born. But his mother never so much as entertained the idea of remarrying, despite her beauty. Her dark hair had no grey, and except for a few laugh lines, his mother was as young and beautiful as she had always been.

"It's the least I can do. You are my son, and you need me," she said, swatting him. "Now, go on with you. I have a few things to do before we receive our guests. Walk with me to my parlor. They are expected in less than an hour. By the way, I received a note from Jeremy. Your brother wanted to surprise us with his return from his tour but thought it might be wiser to warn us in case we were entertaining."

He could not wait to see Jeremy. "If that letter is for him, please tell him we will look for him and keep a place ready for him at dinner. What a wonderful surprise," Alan said. "I will return shortly, Mother. I need to speak to Colin and his brother Johnathan before they leave."

"You men have spent the day closeted up. There must be something cooking," she teased.

He laughed. "No. We've just been catching up. And if you must know, we are discussing my becoming a silent partner in their fencing club. Although, I hold little hope. Colin has all the money he needs, and the club is doing exceedingly well. I'm trying to talk them into expansion."

"You boys have always talked about doing business together. Maybe this will be the one. I'll wish you good fortune on it, son," Lady Hardin said.

"It's not what is on my mind, though, Mother. Uncle Edward's death occupies my thoughts," Alan murmured.

"How so?" His mother took a seat on the blue tapestry settee. "Sit," she said, patting the seat.

"I have not mentioned this to you, Mother, but perhaps I should. I received two notes over the past few weeks and both of them questioned my inheriting the earldom," Alan began. "When I questioned

Travers, I discovered Uncle Edward also received a mysterious note a short while before he had his accident."

"My goodness! That would give anyone pause. What is the magistrate doing to investigate this?" She visibly shook. "It frightens me to think someone might threaten my son."

"Nothing. Truth be told, I have imagined that if Uncle Edward's accident was no accident, I might also become someone's objective." He stood and walked to the window, clasping his hands behind his back. "Things were simpler before I assumed the earldom. Between accepting responsibilities for two young women—one almost too old to be my ward—and now this . . ." He let the sentence drop and gave his head a clearing shake. "Uncle Edward probably dismissed this, as most would have—including me, when I received the first odd note. But to get two and find that he also may have received them changes things. I have spoken to the king's agent, Mr. Ruben. And of course, with my connections to the Crown, I don't plan to leave a stone unturned."

"Well, there is some comfort in that, I suppose," she said, placing her hands in her lap. "Should I also be concerned? What about the Rollins girls?"

He sighed. "I apologize, Mother. Perhaps I should have followed Society's dictates and not worried you about these matters. But I have always benefited from your uncanny ability to spot a problem. You have always been my 'fixer.' Whether it was a skinned knee, or deciding which friend to holiday with at school, you have always given me the benefit of your intuition without expectation. I hope you will give this matter perspective. Maintain a heightened awareness, but don't let it define your day, or I shall regret telling you and adding worries to your already full agenda. The girls' stepmother will be a big enough handful, and you will need your faculties to deal with her antics."

His mother beamed. "I promise not to let it bother me. But knowledge is power, and the more I'm aware of, the better, especially considering your wards."

"Pay close attention to her son, Daniel Chadwick. He shall most likely attend this evening. I'm hoping between the two of us, we can keep him under observation. If we are at two opposite ends of the table, we can monitor him without his being aware."

"You inherited that from your father. You are an excellent judge of character. Go! See your friends and discuss the venture and this matter. I will see to my correspondence. Our guests will be here before too long," his mother said, withdrawing a sheet of vellum.

# CHAPTER 5

THAT EVENING

"*A*re you ready to get dressed, my lady?" Jane asked.

"Oh yes. I fear if I'm in here alone much longer, Delores will take the seat opposite me and ask me to tell her what I've read. She's been extremely attentive today," Elizabeth said. "Sickeningly so," she said under her breath.

"Ha! I heard that, my lady. Careful—the walls around here may have ears. We don't know what she offered others to spy for her— only what she offered me," Jane whispered. "I dare not let her know I told you."

"I understand, believe me," Elizabeth said, picking through her jewelry. She picked up her mother's pearls and lovingly threaded them through her fingers. "I miss you, Mama," she whispered, swiping a rogue tear from her face. "I hate her. Mama told me to never use that word, but I cannot help it. Delores doesn't like Penny, and I fear she has some sick plan up her sleeve where I am concerned." A sick feeling formed in the pit of her stomach as she recalled Daniel's words she had overheard from outside her father's study. She could not share what she had heard . . . with anyone, not even with Jane.

*"Why don't you marry him, Mother? Use the same seduction trap you used with the baron."* Had her stepmother tricked her father into a marriage with pregnancy? Elizabeth barely recalled her stepmother being pregnant. If memory served, she had lost the baby—a boy—a few months after she married her father. Elizabeth had mourned the loss of her baby brother and recalled her stepmother took to her bed for months, despondent over the death of her baby.

"Your stepmother is jealous. Always has been," Jane whispered, as she withdrew the rose-satin evening dress from the wardrobe and hung it on the edge of the door before stepping back to admire it. "Lovely! The rose pink compliments your rich brown hair. Your mama loved you in pink. You are very much like her. She was always happy and beautiful—truly a gentle soul. "

"Why did you say that . . . about the baroness?" Elizabeth asked, tracing her finger down the rich satin of the dress.

Jane remained quiet for a moment before speaking. "Your mama, God rest her, would be horrified at the things that woman has done to her home and the slights she pays her daughters. I'm quiet around her . . . not hard of hearing."

Elizabeth laughed. "I am looking forward to dinner at Lord Halsburg's residence—as long as I don't have to sit at the table with Daniel." Her stepmother had made up no less than three occasions where she stuck her head in Elizabeth's room, asking her how she felt. It was easy to imagine what that was all about. If she had even hinted at a trace of illness, Lady Delores Rollins would cancel the visit under the pretense of family illness. Having witnessed that behavior enough times when her father lived, Elizabeth went out of her way to show herself as hale and looking forward to the evening—always smiling when her stepmother visited.

The woman might have done it anyway, but Elizabeth suspected she was leery of the earl's power over whatever her father had left her and Penny. And she wished she had overheard more between mother and son that morning—something that would have given her an idea of what the earl held in trust for her sister and her. Her stepmother whined about money constantly—something Elizabeth was unaccustomed to.

A tap on the door was all the warning they had got before Lady Rollins glided into the room. She walked to Elizabeth's vanity, where Jane was finishing the last few touches on Elizabeth's hair.

"Elizabeth, you were right about the dress. It is your color and looks nice," Lady Rollins said pointedly, before glancing around the room—as if she had been looking for something but settled on nothing. "We should leave. His lordship will expect us." As she left, she stopped at the door. "Your pearls would look lovely with the dress." Then she left just as quickly as she had entered.

Jane picked up the pearls. "You had laid these out to wear. Shall I help you put them on?"

"Yes, thank you," Elizabeth said, turning around and carefully picking up the cascade of curls Jane had created. *How odd for her to recommend my mother's pearls to me.*

Jane fastened the pearls, and Elizabeth slowly lowered the curls. "I suppose I'm ready."

THE RIDE to the earl's house was short and quiet, except for the clopping sound of the horses' hooves on the cobblestone bricks. Elizabeth sat with Penny, facing her stepmother and stepbrother. Nary a sound passed between them in the stale air of the carriage. When they arrived, a smartly uniformed footman stepped out to open the door, and Daniel stepped out first without waiting for his mother. *Daniel has the manners of a goat*, she thought.

As she waited for Penny to depart the carriage, she heard the earl stop him at the door. "Welcome to Halsburg House, Mr. Chadwick, Lady Rollins. Please allow James to escort you to the parlor where my mother awaits. I will follow with your lovely daughters, Lady Rollins.

When she and Penny emerged from the carriage, Elizabeth looked up into the eyes of her very handsome guardian and her heart did a strange flip.

"Welcome, ladies," the earl said, stepping between them and extending his arms. "My mother and I are happy to see you both." He leaned over and kissed Elizabeth's gloved hand, sending a fissure of feeling up and down her neck.

"Thank you, my lord," Penny and Elizabeth said together.

She caught herself staring at the earl, so Elizabeth focused on the steps to avoid embarrassment. When last they met, she had focused more on what he was saying—he was to be her new guardian after the death of her father's best friend, a man she had called 'uncle' most of her life. Of course, there was no actual relation to the man, but he had always been kind and generous to both her and Penny. Losing him had been like losing the last link to her father—so she hadn't seen the man in front of her, at least not as she saw him today. She couldn't fathom having a guardian who couldn't have been over five years her senior. And one that looked like him . . . *so handsome.*

"Ladies," he said, escorting them into the drawing room. "Allow me to introduce you to my mother, Lady Hardin."

A beautiful, dark-haired woman stood with her back to them while speaking to Elizabeth's stepmother. Upon hearing her name, she spun around and, with a warm smile on her face, walked to them. Both girls dipped in a curtsey. "These are two lovely young ladies, son," she gushed. "I am sure we will get on famously."

Approvingly, Elizabeth took in the rich burgundy and dark wood tones of the rooms. It was beautifully appointed with navy blue and gold-toned accents. The room's masculinity fit Lord Halsburg perfectly.

"You must be Mr. Chadwick," Lord Halsburg said, extending a hand to Daniel, who stood next to a burgundy couch. "Pleased to meet you."

She gave a side glance and noticed the earl was looking her way. But it was her stepbrother's expression that caught her breath. Daniel looked angry. Thankfully, he remained over there, unable to walk away from the conversation with the earl. Whatever they were discussing, Daniel looked like he had become animated, with his attention focused on the earl. While she couldn't make out what they were saying, Elizabeth caught herself eavesdropping, mesmerized by the warm, rich tenor of Lord Halsburg's voice, and perplexed by the way it soothed her.

"Would you care for a glass of sherry or lemonade?" Lady Hardin asked, drawing her from her musings. With an effervescent smile, the woman gave Penny a quick wink before giving a slight nod to the attending footman to serve drinks.

Lord Halsburg's mother edged closer to Elizabeth and Penny, who stood near their stepmother. "Lord Halsburg has asked me to commission seasonal clothing for you both. I hope you don't mind, but I made appointments with Madame Trousseau. She looks forward to meeting you."

Elizabeth heard Penny inhale and smiled. This was just what Penny needed. Her sister had outgrown her wardrobe, and Delores had forced her to wear out-of-date dresses, hemmed, like today, so they would fall to the right length. She could not disappoint her sister. Elizabeth nodded. "Thank you, Lady Hardin. We have never been to Madame Trousseau's establishment and look forward to that."

With a warm smile, Lady Hardin clasped her hands and turned to their stepmother. "This will be delightful. You will, of course, attend, won't you, Lady Rollins? Madame Trousseau would be happy for you to commission a new frock for the holidays."

Had Elizabeth not already swallowed her sherry, she feared she might have choked. It seemed clear the earl had indeed discovered someone had canceled their modiste appointments. This trip was his way of letting Lady Rollins know. She was starting to adore her guardian.

"I would expect Lady Delores Rollins will pay for her own dresses," At the covert glance Lady Hardin gave her son at the mention of the visit to Madame Trousseau's establishment, Elizabeth wondered if her stepmother's recent trip to the dressmaker had been billed to the earl. Her stepmother's lips puckered as if she had just swallowed a sour pickle. "Well, certainly, I shall love to attend. I will need to assist my lovely . . . daughters," she finished dryly.

"Excellent," his mother said demurely, with a broad smile. "With

Christmastide almost upon us, I took a chance and scheduled it for tomorrow afternoon. I hope that time will work for everyone."

Elizabeth noticed Penny nodding, so she smiled and nodded as well. A side glance at her stepmother showed the woman looking slightly befuddled and stalling on her reply. This would be an interesting outing.

"You will come with us, won't you, Lady Rollins? It won't be the same without you," Lady Hardin prodded sweetly.

"Y . . . yes of course! I look forward to it. Your kind gesture caught me unawares, that is all," her stepmother replied, forcing a smile. "It will be a grand outing!" she cooed.

"I have arranged a light luncheon at the restaurant next to Madame Trousseau's, and of course, we must stop and get an ice at Gunter's. It will be such a wonderful girl's day!"

A footman entered the room. "Dinner is served."

"Shall we?" Lady Hardin said to Penny. Penny nodded and the two of them walked into the room, followed by her stepmother, escorted by Earl Halsburg. Daniel held out his arm, and Elizabeth reluctantly accepted it.

"It's my pleasure, Elizabeth," he said with a wicked grin. "This should prove an interesting dinner."

Elizabeth feigned a smile but focused her attention on her tall, handsome guardian, refusing to respond. Luckily, Lady Hardin had arranged seating, and Elizabeth found herself seated at the right-hand side of the earl. Strangely, a tremor of excitement worked its way down her arms and across her shoulders, as she covertly studied the man next to her. The scuffing of a chair against the table pulled her attention to Daniel, who found his place marker across from Elizabeth.

"This is a pretty room, isn't it, Stepmother?" Penny said, happily taking her seat next to Lady Hardin, while her stepmother seated herself to the right of Lady Hardin.

As they worked their way through the first course of the meal, the conversation focused on the upcoming girls' day—mostly on Penny's excitement as she kept discussing the excursion. Her sister's excitement was so contagious, her stepmother began to contribute ideas about their outing—a shocking development.

Oddly, a vacant dinner plate sat between her and Penny. While she noticed it, Elizabeth felt no urge to comment on it. *However, Daniel did —with a mouthful of food.*

"Who's the plate for?" he asked, nodding to the plate between his two stepsisters, in between bites of buttered bread.

Elizabeth made it a practice not to look in his direction at the table, or she would leave hungry. She set her soup spoon down and stared into the bowl, biting her lower lip to avoid smiling. From beneath her lashes, she noticed her stepmother had done the same, unwilling to take credit for her son's lack of etiquette.

"I apologize for not saying something earlier," the earl said, smoothly. "My younger brother, Jeremy, is on his way home. We've instructed the servants to leave a place setting for dinners in case he joins us during our meal. I was reluctant to alter it."

As if on cue, someone cleared their throat from the doorway. "Ahem."

"Jeremy!" Lady Hardin said, excitedly turning to see him. "My goodness, we had not known when to expect you, but hoped for your return every day, as you can see." She pointed to the setting.

"Do not stand, Mother. I expected to make it here at dinnertime as a surprise and changed at my last stop. But I apologize for interrupting your dinner party."

"Nonsense! Allow me to introduce you. These are our friends, Lady Rollins, and her son, Mr. Daniel Chadwick," Lady Hardin said.

"And there are her stepdaughters, who are also my wards, Miss Elizabeth Rollins and her sister, Miss Penny Rollins," Alan added.

Jeremy arched a brow, and a knowing look passed between the brothers before Jeremy took a seat—a look Elizabeth didn't miss.

"Lady Rollins is the widow of Baron George Rollins, Uncle Edward's good friend, correct?" Jeremy asked. He gave her a curt bow. "My uncle spoke fondly of your husband. Whenever Alan or I visited, they were always together, it seemed. We grew up knowing your husband, almost like an additional uncle. He is missed."

41

"Thank you, my lord. I was unaware of that. I know he considered your uncle his dearest friend—almost a brother," Lady Rollins said, glancing between the earl and his brother. Giving what appeared to be an honest smile, she added. "You boys look the epitome of night and day! I'll bet you have heard that often."

Lady Hardin laughed. "Yes! My eldest gets his coloring from me and Jeremy from his father."

Indeed, Jeremy looked the opposite of his brother, except in height. Both men stood approximately six feet, Elizabeth thought, judging from their being as tall as the door openings, which were noticeably larger than those in her house. Her guardian was the most handsome man she had ever met, but his brother was a close second. The earl's dark hair and grey eyes contrasted with his younger brother's short blond waves and brown eyes.

The commentary seemed to relax everyone as the second course was served. "I only missed the turtle soup," remarked Jeremy. He held his hand up to the footman, who started to serve it. "If you don't mind, James, I will pass. I've had lots of soup on my tour."

"As you wish, sir," he said and left the room, taking the soup tureen back to the kitchen.

"I had hoped to make it back in time for dinner. I did not know we would have such lovely guests," Jeremy said, giving a meaningful look at his brother.

"I thought it would be an excellent opportunity to reintroduce myself to the baroness and her family." Alan turned to the baroness. "I asked my mother to assist me with the things young ladies need—clothing, dancing lessons, a governess, and instructors for painting and other special activities."

The baroness opened her mouth to say something closed it and then opened it again. "I see," she said tightly. "I can perfectly manage my household, my lord, and that includes the needs you mentioned."

"I'm sure you can agree I should oversee their financial needs and ensure their activities are directed in the proper, intended direction through personal observation—in which, I am asking my mother to serve in my stead when it makes the most sense." He paused meaningfully. "I believe this will work effectively. Of course, we shall consult with you on certain matters—for example, the time and place of their lessons." His voice was gentle but firm.

"I would be pleased to provide direction for the girls, as I have been doing, my lord. Elizabeth is nearly too old to be considered a ward—and you are only a few years her senior. This is highly unusual," the baroness sputtered.

"I agree on both counts, Lady Rollins. Miss Elizabeth is coming of age in a matter of months."

Elizabeth's face heated, unsure of how to behave, as they talked about her as if she was not in the room.

"Your husband charged me to make financial decisions for his daughters and see to their needs." The earl gave a meaningful pause and glanced at Elizabeth before continuing. "Partly for the reasons you just named, I will ensure Miss Elizabeth Rollins has a London Season beginning in April. In the meantime, I would welcome your help, but Miss Elizabeth has been out of mourning for some time and could not take part in the last Season. I intend that both Miss Elizabeth and Miss Penny stay in London for the duration of the Season. Mother has agreed to chaperone Elizabeth and help her navigate her way back into Society. And I plan to move Lady Penny's governess to our townhouse once the bedrooms we want them to use are suitably rehabilitated."

Elizabeth caught a flash of surprise cross Lady Hardin's face before it broke into a smile.

The baroness shook her head. "No. The girls cannot leave. You assured me last year when you assumed their guardianship that they would stay in the house."

Her stepmother's concern was not for them leaving; it was the loss of income the woman would have for the upkeep of her household if Elizabeth and Penny moved to Lord Halsburg's townhouse.

Fortunately, their footman came in with a course change, and while everyone was preoccupied with the delivery of the new course, Elizabeth looked over at the earl and caught his gaze. "Lord Halsburg, could we speak? Perhaps after dinner?" She spoke in guarded tones, hoping not to draw Daniel's attention.

The earl smiled at her. "Of course, Lady Elizabeth."

He rested a hand near hers—barely touching—but enough to send waves of excitement to Elizabeth's midsection.

"Allow me to stop by the parlor following the meal and we can find a few minutes to speak," he said, staring into her eyes.

"Thank you, my lord," Elizabeth returned.

A shiver shook her as Elizabeth looked across the table and noticed Daniel listening to the conversation around him and wearing a slight smirk.

Elizabeth was determined to protect her sister. She refused to allow Daniel Chadwick to have the upper hand. As she ate, she mulled over her question. The earl had been sending an agreed-upon amount of maintenance for Penny and herself. If he planned to move them here, she would speak to the earl about allowing Jane and Miss Mary to come, too. Her stepmother had threatened often enough to discharge her maid over what she cost to keep.

Ten minutes later, his mother stood. "Ladies, why don't we withdraw to the parlor?"

Elizabeth removed to the parlor with Lady Hardin, Penny, and the baroness. She noticed James stop Lady Hardin and hand her a message, but thought nothing of it.

About ten minutes later, the earl stopped by the parlor. "May I speak with Miss Rollins?" he asked his mother, giving a slight nod in Elizabeth's direction. "I promise to bring her right back, unharmed. If your maid can follow, that would be helpful."

"Of course, son."

He waited for Elizabeth and Martha, his mother's maid. They walked to his study and he offered her a seat. Martha took a seat across the room, in front of the fireplace, and waited. "My lord, I didn't want to pull you away from your company."

"Nonsense. I am here for you and your sister. How can I help you?"

"I had a question but could not feel comfortable asking it at dinner," she said softly.

"Perfectly understandable. Does your stepbrother always stare at you? I noticed he did that quite a bit," the earl said.

"Yes . . . and it's disconcerting. But in my household, there is not much I can do. He is . . . unsettling. And that's part of what I want to speak with you about. He was banned from our house by my father years ago for molesting one of the staff. I do not know why he is back, but I fear for our safety with him," she began.

"Has he made any inappropriate gestures?"

"No. He has not, other than his disturbing way of showing up when unexpected and getting too close when he wants to speak with me. It is my sister, Penny, I am most concerned about. She is impressionable and young. Without my father in the house, I fear for us. I recall you mentioning moving us to your townhouse, and I wanted to ask if you would also take my lady's maid and Penny's governess."

"The governess your stepmother fired?"

So he knew. She wasn't surprised. "Yes."

"Our cooks are friends. Yes. I will bring them both. And we plan to move you here when the rooms are finished being refurbished."

He touched her back. "You are trembling."

"Only because I heard Daniel's voice in the hallway. I fear he was outside the door eavesdropping."

"I will make sure he doesn't bother you, Miss Elizabeth. It was my mother's idea to move you. But it makes sense. It's an immense home and with a proper chaperone, there is no reason you cannot move into my townhome."

"Please, call me Elizabeth. It seems too formal. You are my guardian, after all."

# CHAPTER 6

THE NEXT DAY

*A*lan met his brother on the stairs, heading to the drawing room. "You must have the same thought as me." He laughed. "I'm starving."

"I'm hungry, too." Jeremy laughed too. "Last night's dinner held more excitement than most. I'm afraid I left more on my plate than I should have."

"I knew it could get tense but had not planned to come away from it hungry," Alan confessed.

"I'm rather happy I didn't miss out on your guests, even though I felt bad about interrupting your party. You have your hands full with that family, dear brother. Not the young ladies, but the stepmother and her son."

"I'm beginning to see that," Alan said, opening the door to the drawing room. "I could use your opinion on some things. The whole situation has me irritated," Alan confessed, lowering his voice. "I had no wish for any of this. Yet, I'm drowning in conflict."

"Whoa, where is this coming from, brother?" Jeremy asked, patting

his brother on the back. "I watched you last evening. You took a difficult situation and hit it head-on. I take it the baroness has been skim-
ming from the girls and they are not getting what they need." He held
his hand up when the footman moved to serve them. "We've got this,
James."

"Thank you, Mr. Hardin."

Alan filled his plate with eggs, rashers, and toast and sat down,
where he noticed James had placed his mother's broadsheet and his
newspaper. "It seems we beat Mother this morning," he observed,
laughing.

"She's most likely getting dressed for the shopping trip. Do you
think the baroness will go?" Jeremy asked.

"I don't think so," Alan supposed. "I believe she realized we were
on to her antics. I almost found it hard to conduct myself as a gentleman, and at the same time, ensure she knows I was serious where my
wards are concerned."

"Yes . . . your wards," teased Jeremy. "Elizabeth is quite a beauty.
And her younger sister holds great promise to be one as well. She's
fourteen and already a lovely young lady."

Alan couldn't reconcile with the pang of jealousy that shot through
him at his brother's mention of Elizabeth. True, he had looked in her
direction when he thought no one had seen him, but her auburn
brown hair and soft curls were the perfect frames for her large green
eyes. They were almost a blue-green, something he could not recall
ever seeing on a woman before. *How had he not remembered the color of
her eyes until last night?*

"Did I lose you, brother?" Jeremy teased.

"I'm sorry. I was thinking of something from last night," Alan
quickly amended.

"Of course," Jeremy said superciliously, as he poured himself a
glass of tea.

"Be serious, Jeremy," Alan chided, good-humoredly. "I do,
however, think you have grasped the situation, exactly. I hated to
strong-arm the situation, but I feel the only attachment the baroness
has to these girls is to their inheritance." Alan indicated to his

brother to sit next to him, as they walked to the sideboard and took a plate.

"Do you plan to move the ladies here?" Jeremy asked. "Mother has always wanted a daughter. Don't you think you are playing with matches here?"

"What do you mean?" Alan asked.

"I cannot think you do not see the attraction," Jeremy said.

"No. I am her guardian. It is my job to maintain her safety," Alan said, shaking his head and hoping to clear it of images of Miss Elizabeth Rollins. "That's the reason I've asked Mother to chaperone her."

"I see," Jeremy said astutely. "With no male heir, Mother said the barony went back to the Crown. Something makes little sense. Rollins had lots of money, didn't he?"

"I see where you are going with this. And yes, he had a lot of money. According to my solicitor—who was also the baron's—the baron changed his will shortly before his death, making Uncle Edward the guardian of his daughters. About six months before his death. The baron reduced Daniel's inheritance to only a small allowance. His wife got a third of his estate, which was substantial. He had investments in the East India Company, as well as excellent returns on others."

"Which begs the question, why is she so worried about money?" mused Jeremy.

"Exactly. I got a bill from her modiste dated the day she was supposed to take the girls for a new wardrobe. Yet, when my valet questioned her, Everly said the modiste denied taking any orders for the girls, short of a new pelisse and hat—outerwear—for each of them. Mother noticed Penny's dress last evening was out of style for a child her age." He shook his head. "Elizabeth has less than six months before her twenty-first birthday when she will leave my guardianship. I owe it to her to make sure she and her sister are treated decently—as her father intended."

"She is beautiful," Jeremy observed. "Miss Elizabeth."

"Yes, she is," Alan said. A smile formed on his lips. "Very true. I tried to handle the guardianship from a distance, but as you've noticed, that didn't work. Miss Elizabeth has poise and a sense of herself I don't see in the cloying debutantes. I suspect it could be her learned sensitivity to her stepsibling and stepparent. It's obvious to me that the baroness does only what's needed. She has no feelings for her husband's daughters. And I can't get a good read on her relationship with her son." *Miss Elizabeth also has the most beautiful eyes I have ever seen*, he thought.

"He's vulgar," Lady Hardin said, walking into the room. Her sons stood as James pulled out her chair. After she sat, the footman filled her cup with tea and brought her a plate of food. "Thank you, James. That will be all."

"Mother, what time do you plan to leave for your excursion with my wards?" Alan asked, changing the subject.

"At ten o'clock," she replied, applying some sugar to her tea. "It should be an interesting day."

"My guess is the baroness will back out," Jeremy offered. "Her ill intentions towards the girls were fairly exposed during dinner."

"I hope so, although a part of me wanted to observe the interaction between them. I am confused why she would divert money intended for the girls for her purpose."

James reentered the room. "My lord, Mr. Ruben is here to see you."

"Show him in, James," Alan instructed.

"Good morning, Mr. Ruben. Join us. James, can you get him a plate?"

"Yes, my lord," the footman said, filling a plate from the sideboard and placing it before their guest, and stepping from the room.

Alan laid down his fork. "It's good to see you, Ruben. Let me introduce my brother, Mr. Jeremy Hardin."

Ruben dipped his head. "Nice to have your acquaintance, sir."

"Have your investigations revealed anything?" Alan asked.

"Not on your uncle's death," he said. "However, I uncovered some rather interesting information on Mr. Chadwick."

"Do tell," Lady Hardin said, setting her teacup on the table.

"He has been accruing debts all over London, but since his stepfather's death, his credit has experienced a renewal, of sorts—until a few weeks ago. And he's a terrible gambler. Drinks excessively and never wins. After the baron's death, perhaps coincidentally, he seemed to have a more fluent flow of cash at his disposal. But the tap seems to have waned again."

"Do you think someone was financing him?" Alan asked.

"I believe his mother was his banker," Ruben said. "But it's my belief she didn't realize it until recently. That could be the reason she moved him home."

"How could he have his hands in her money without her knowledge?" Jeremy asked.

"I have no certain answer to that, but I suspect he stole from his mother," Ruben said.

Lady Hardin audibly sucked in her breath.

"Banknotes paid most of the debt. I think he might have taken them, somehow. But word has it, she cut him off, completely, forcing his move back home," Ruben explained while glancing around the room. "And there's something else. Miss Elizabeth Rollins' name was floated when he was deep in his cup one night, according to a source."

Alan felt a surge of protectiveness he had not expected. "That's ludicrous. He is her *stepbrother*," he shouted, seeing Elizabeth Rollins' face in his mind. She was innocent, and he was responsible for her. Perhaps that was the reason she kept intruding on his thoughts.

"Alan?" his mother prodded softly. Both his mother and Jeremy were watching him.

"Sorry, I was just thinking about what you were telling me," he apologized.

"My Lord, the man is unscrupulous and holds no loyalty to anyone but himself. While she is his stepsister, he apparently feels no brotherly love in her direction. We will let nothing happen to the girl," Ruben said.

"How can you be certain?" Jeremy asked. "He has free rein and lives in the same house with the girls."

"I can change that," Alan asserted without thinking, slightly perplexed as to his roiling gut and the anger he felt. He would not retract it. He meant it. If that was the only way he could make sure she and her sister were safe, he would move her into his house.

"I believe we should take our time on this, Alan," Lady Hardin said, placing her hand on the table next to her son's. She looked at Ruben. "We have discussed this, and to that end, have rooms being redecorated for the girls."

"Keep an eye on things," Ruben cautioned. "Of all I heard, that disturbed me. It appeared he was attempting to damage her reputation. But to what end?"

"Oh, I can think of what end. If he ruins her, he will have to marry her," Jeremy asserted.

"No! Surely, he would not do that to . . ." Lady Hardin began.

"A stepsister?" Alan interrupted. "Jeremy may be right. They banned the man from the house when he was barely fifteen and sent him to school. He spent his holidays with friends, one supposes. When he became of age, I'm sure the baron gave him a suitable income, but he spent it gaming, drinking, and . . . on other pleasures," Alan finished.

"I am perfectly aware of what he did," his mother appended. "And I'm in total agreement that these girls should move here. But first, you must establish a relationship with them, son," Lady Hardin interjected. "Today would be a splendid opportunity to do that. Why don't you and your brother meet us for lunch at the Fatted Snail Restaurant? It would be an opportunity to relax and get to know your wards."

"You make a good point, Mother. As I have nothing else scheduled for today, I will be glad to join you," Alan agreed.

Mr. Ruben withdrew his pocket watch from his waistcoat and checked the time. "I hate to end our time together, but I must meet the man I've assigned to watch the Rollins' townhouse." Standing, he pocketed his watch.

Alan stood and shook his hand. "Thank you for coming and updating us. Alert me to anything you turn up on my uncle's accident. I will walk you to the door."

"Certainly, my lord," Ruben said. He gave a swift bow to Lady Hardin and left the room with her son.

THE DOOR CLOSED, and Jeremy leaned back in the chair and watched his mother move the remains of her food around her plate. She piddled with stuff when she was planning or thinking through things. "I know what you are doing, Mother. And it won't work," Jeremy said.

"I cannot know what you are inferring," his mother said, giving a coy smile.

"You hope to strike up more than a familiarity between my brother and Miss Rollins," Jeremy said.

"I am sure I don't know what you are speaking of. And even if what you say had a dribble of merit, one cannot control another person's sense of attraction to another," she replied.

"True. You are counting on Alan being blinded by . . . his attraction to his ward. That is something he will fight if indeed he feels it. We both know you have always wanted a daughter and with these two wards, you might have found yourself at least one to cater to. Miss Rollins will be in the marriage mart soon enough."

"True," she said. "And if she found your brother interesting, who are we to quibble with whom a person finds attractive?"

"This scheme could backfire. You realize that?" Jeremy said.

"Fine! I'm dabbling a bit. But I see it as 'encouragement.' I can count on your . . . discretion, can't I, son?" She gave him a meaningful look.

"Certainly. You have my word."

"Good. Then I can count on seeing you at the restaurant at lunch." She laid her broadsheet back on the table and took a final sip of her tea. Standing, she gave a slight jerk to her skirt, displacing the wrinkles, and left the room."

"My homecoming has been entertaining, to say the least," he murmured. "I should think today's luncheon will only add to my enjoyment."

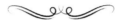

ELIZABETH'S DAY began with her sister bounding into her room.

"Wake up, sleepyhead!" Penny said, springing onto the bed. "Lizbeth, I am so excited! I am so happy to get new clothes. It's been forever since I've had a new dress! Did you like the earl? I liked the earl. And his brother was handsome! Don't you think so?"

Elizabeth rose from her bed to see her sister swirl around in a circle, holding her nightgown as if it was a ballgown and she was a princess. "Whoa! One thought at a time. I'm still dusting the cobwebs from my brain," she said, tweaking her sister's nose.

"But didn't you like the earl? I saw him watching you. And that dreadful Daniel was watching. I hope he will leave soon," Penny droned.

"Yes, I do like the earl. I'll admit, he was much more engaging than the first time we met. Which was at Uncle Edward's funeral," she said, realizing that was probably why his character had seemed rather sedate. It had been a funeral. "And yes! I'm excited for you! Jane told me she had added matching fabric to the bottom of your dresses to hem them. Have I answered all your questions?" Elizabeth playfully ticked off imaginary questions on her fingers.

"No! You left off the part about his brother. Jeremy! He was so handsome."

"And you are so young! Yes, he is attractive. And since you have sort of claimed him," she teased, "it wouldn't be right for your sister to also remark on his looks."

"Yes, you can. You just cannot touch!" Penny said playfully.

"Penny! I think you have been sneaking into my romance novels. I must remember to check under your bed!" Elizabeth replied, laughing.

The door opened and Jane entered with a tray of biscuits and chocolate. "Miss Mary told me your sister had abandoned her for breakfast, so I added some biscuits to your tray," she said, smiling. "You two should get ready. Lady Hardin will be here in an hour."

"Can we sit in front of your fire and eat, Lizbeth?" Penny asked, excited.

"Of course, Penny! And we can plot out our day," Elizabeth replied. She adored her little sister and wanted the best of everything for her. Since Papa died, she had done her best to shield Penny from Delores and her viciousness, but it had been impossible. Her stepmother's wrath knew no bounds. When she had fired Miss Mary, Elizabeth had felt her temper boil, but before she had said anything, apparently the woman had realized the earl would step in, so she had rehired the governess.

*Penny and I must get away from this house*, she realized. Perhaps she should take this shopping trip seriously. The Earl of Halsburg's mother mentioned they were having some rooms refurbished. So that was an option. Or, if she found someone to marry, perhaps the earl would allow Penny to live with her. "But first I need to find a husband," she murmured. And that lent even more importance to the shopping trip ahead of them. There had been a couple of suitors before her father died, but his death had left her numb, and she had stopped taking their calls. Oh, if she had only had a crystal ball and could have seen into the future, she might have done things differently, she thought miserably.

*No, you wouldn't,* a voice in her head said.

"Let's get ready, Penny, dear! We shall make this a wonderful day and have lots of fun. I cannot wait to see what fabrics we can find for you. Just think! You will have all new clothes!" Something her younger sister should have had all along.

# CHAPTER 7

"*T*his color goes fabulously with your unusual eyes, Miss Elizabeth," Lady Hardin said, fingering the azure satin. "Madame Trousseau has a wonderful selection of fabrics."

"I have always gravitated towards the blues and deep rose pinks, but don't recall ever having a dress made from this color," Elizabeth added approvingly.

"Oh, *oui*! I love ze color on you, Miss Rollins. It is lovely. You and your sister are so lovely," Madame Trousseau said, walking up behind them. "If you don't mind, I would like to help ze little sister select some fabrics."

"Oh yes! Thank you." Elizabeth watched the modiste take Penny aside and show her fabrics. "Thank you, Lady Hardin," she said, facing her benefactor. "This is most generous of you and your son."

"Pish!" She waved her hand dismissively. "Think nothing of it! Your father was my husband's brother's dearest friend. Edward would have insisted, Miss Rollins."

"Please call me Elizabeth or even Liz. My friends called me Liz."

"I have always loved the name Elizabeth, so I shall call you that," Lady Hardin said. Her eyes narrowed slightly. "What do you mean *called*?"

Elizabeth sucked in her breath, feeling suddenly squeamish. She had not meant to call attention to her and Penny's virtual isolation from their friends. "Since Papa's death, my stepmother prefers that my friends *not* visit."

"Really, Elizabeth? She *said* that?" Lady Hardin's shock was clear. "But *why?*"

"Yes. She asked that we not have guests in the house." Lady Hardin's features hardened.

"Elizabeth, what about you visiting your friends?" His mother persisted. "Surely, she did not forbid that."

Elizabeth found she liked Lady Hardin. The woman was a force—*a supportive force*. It was nice to have someone she could talk to again. It had been so long since she'd had someone who cared about her inner-most thoughts. Father had loved her, but their relationship had been different than her mother's relationship with her. Elizabeth had been fourteen when Mama died. Except for Jane, there had been few other females in her life. "I used to visit my friends, but when I returned, I would find my room disturbed. Things were moved. And worse, pieces of jewelry my father had given me went missing . . . little by little. They were special pieces that my mother wore every day—including Mama's sapphire wedding ring and a gold necklace with a locket that had a small painting of her and my father on their wedding day. I suppose they were more sentimental than valuable."

"That's terrible. I recall seeing the locket around your mother's neck when she visited," Lady Hardin replied.

"Of course, I could not point fingers. When I realized it happened only when I left the house, I resolved to stay home. When her . . . irritation . . . extended to Penny, I was glad I was home to buffer Penny. Lady Rollins and I occasionally have appointments together, but when they occur, nothing is disturbed."

Lady Hardin pursed her lips. "The intrusion into your room happened *before* your stepbrother moved to the household?"

"Yes, but please do not worry. Since I limit my excursions, my room has stayed . . . intact," Elizabeth explained. She found it freeing to finally say something about this harassment—and theft.

"What about today? The baroness chose not to come. Will that be a problem?" the earl's mother asked.

"No. I took precautions and hid my jewelry in my sister's room. It is a secret hiding place I found as a child when I lived in the nursery. I don't think Penny knows about it," Elizabeth said.

"I should not say this, but my head wants to explode! I would never have thought her capable—or anyone capable—of such devilry. My son is your guardian. Bring your jewelry to our town-house, and we shall keep it there for you. If I have my way, you will move from that house. *Her treatment of you and your sister is awful.*"

"Madame, I see you have selected the aqua mist satin," Madame Trousseau said, approaching them. "Would you like to have a dress made in that? I could suggest a beautiful overlay for it."

"Do you like it?" Lady Hardin asked.

"I do. I have always had a propensity for the rose pinks, but this has my attention," Elizabeth said, loving the fabric. "I would love a dress from that material."

"Lizbeth, what do you think of these pink silks?" Penny asked, holding up a bolt of pink.

"I love them for you. Blondes look gorgeous in pink," Elizabeth said, kissing her sister on the cheek.

Penny selected a bolt of pale blue fabric, holding it close to her body, as she peered into the looking glass. "Lizbeth, I feel like Cinderella!" she exclaimed, giving a slight twirl. "Lady Hardin, you are like a fairy godmother!"

"My dear, you have excellent taste in fabrics. We shall take all of them," Lady Hardin said, giving Penny a quick hug. "Don't forget the matching ribbons for your hair!" She turned to the modiste, who stood next to the seamstress holding a stack of fabric bolts. "Madame, please have dresses made from all the fabrics these young women have selected." She showed the stack of fabric bolts on the counter. "I'd like ten dresses for each one of them, and something in green for Miss Rollins for the Christmas holiday and one in gold for Miss Penny. Add in all the ribbons and undergarments my ladies have selected. James will be here to pick up the boxes. Put them on my son's tab."

"Yes, my lady. I shall have these boxed up and ready for your footman," Madame Trousseau said.

"No, my lady. That's too much. We don't require that many new dresses," Elizabeth protested. "A few should do us fine."

"Nonsense. You will attend functions with me, and you need several changes of clothes. And Penny deserves just as many." She gazed at the clock on the corner of the counter. "If we are to make lunch on time, we must move on to Wood and select shoes to match the dresses we've commissioned. And then, of course, to the milliners."

"I have never been to Wood to select shoes. What a grand treat," gushed Elizabeth. She rarely got excited about shopping, but to have several shoes matched for her dresses was thrilling.

"Not only will you select shoes, but you will also pick out new half-boots," Lady Hardin said. "My sons are planning to meet us for lunch. And I've arranged for a local chop house to serve us lunch in a private dining room."

"What fun!" Penny exclaimed. "I'm going to always remember this day, forever! Lady Hardin, you are like a fairy godmother straight out of *Cinderella*!"

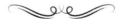

"GENTLEMEN, we'd better break this up. Little brother and I have a lunch meeting with our mother," Alan said, pushing back from the table at the club. Their visit with Shefford and Nelson at the club had been both enlightening and profitable. Jeremy wanted to hear all about *En Garde,* and when Alan mentioned the situation with his wards, he and Jeremy found out Daniel Chadwick had applied to the fencing club. Shefford promised to share the information after Ruben had done his background check. There was something about the man that alarmed Alan—more than just the way he stalked his stepsister, he told himself. *I'm making Chadwick my business.*

"I know you must get back to Lady Shefford. Please give the countess my wishes for a happy festive season," Alan told Shefford, clapping him on the back as they walked from the building. He and Jeremy both shook Jonathan's hand, promising to meet him at the fencing club the following week. It excited Alan to test his skills. It had been a long time since he had fenced.

"Alan," Jeremy said, signaling their coach. "If we don't get to the restaurant, we will endure Mother's wrath. No doubt she has something up her sleeve."

"You are joining your wards for lunch . . . with your mother," Shefford observed. "My money is she has something long-term in mind." He laughed.

"His ward is an exquisite woman," added Jeremy, nudging him in the ribs.

"You are not being helpful, little brother. Ha! I know what you gentlemen are hinting . . . and I won't take the bait," Alan said, laughing.

The coach stopped in front of them. "Can we give you a lift?" Alan asked.

"No, our club is just a few blocks away. A brisk walk will do us good after two glasses of brandy," Shefford teased.

They shook hands, and he and Jeremy entered the coach. As they drew closer to the restaurant, Jeremy pointed to the corner across the street from the eatery. Daniel Chadwick was meeting with another man—passing him something.

"Stop," Alan hit the roof with his cane, stopping the vehicle. He and Jeremy exited and walked to the corner, but Chadwick had disappeared.

"Damnit! Do you think he saw the carriage? We should have brought the unmarked one," Jeremy said.

"Mother took that one. There they are." A carriage stopped across the street and the ladies exited. Jeremy and Alan made their way across. "Hello, ladies," Alan said.

"We were afraid we'd be late," Jeremy said.

"No, my dears. We found the smartest hats in the milliners, and it took a little longer than we had expected. But all is well since we are here together."

Jeremy extended his arm to his mother while Alan extended his to Elizabeth, while Penny followed behind them with the footman into the restaurant.

The door opened and the owner—a short, balding man with large black eyes and a warm smile—met them at the door. Before extending his hand, he rubbed his hands, as if drying them, against a brown apron—that gave minimum cover to a rumpled white shirt. "Welcome to the *Fatted Snail*, Lady Hardin, Lord Halsburg, Mr. Hardin, ladies. I'm Mr. Potter and 'tis my and m'wife's pleasure and privilege to host yer lunch. Your room has been prepared; please follow me." Mr. Potter led them through a short hall, moving past the main dining room where tables of rowdy patrons and the loud clinking of dishes made hearing difficult, coming to a private dining room with a roaring fireplace and a large wooden table in the center of a well-appointed room. The floor was wooden but clean, and sconces lit up the walls. "The missus will be here in a few minutes to take ye orders."

When the door closed behind Potter, Alan looked at his mother. "This looks to be a significant find, Mother. Admittedly, I was unsure of where the *Fatted Snail* was located. It's rare to see ladies eating in town."

His mother beamed. "Of course! I met Mr. Potter ages ago. Your father and I always found his food to be very good. He's shown a desire to develop a restaurant that caters to men and women. Maybe that will happen one day, and private rooms won't be as necessary."

"I don't see that happening," Jeremy said. "Women of means will not appreciate eating among such ruckus."

His mother made a dismissive gesture. "Pish! This is not a ruckus in here. You do not imagine the possibilities. Women don't want to end their shopping trips just to gain sustenance. It's a very simple thing. I think a restaurant would be successful," Lady Hardin said.

"I do, as well," Elizabeth added. "Maybe one day, there will be family restaurants."

Elizabeth Rollins' comment was unexpected but allowed him to change the subject. "How was your shopping venture?" Alan asked.

"I believe we were wildly successful," his mother said, wearing a pleased smile.

The door opened, and Mrs. Potter entered with a teapot and cups. She distributed them among the five guests. "We have pot roast and potatoes with a salad," she offered.

"It is the agreed-upon menu. I hope it shall suit everyone." Lady Hardin said, nodding to Mrs. Potter to serve. The proprietress left to retrieve the meals. "It was the best I could pull together in such a short period and is one of their specialties."

"You mean, besides the fatted snails?" Jeremy asked, grinning.

"Something like that," his mother chided while Mrs. Potter was out of the room.

"I thought this would be a wonderful way to end such a perfect outing," his mother said. "But there is one issue the housekeeper raised, and I hope you will not mind my discussing it here, son. But the boxes for boxing day must be prepared. I was hoping these ladies wouldn't mind helping us do that."

"We haven't had boxing day since my father died. I would be happy to help," Elizabeth said.

"I'd enjoy helping as well," said Penny.

"Then, it's settled. Once we get them put together, we will need to get them to our manor home, but that's something I can have Travers help me with," his mother said, smiling, obviously pleased.

"Elizabeth, I hope you are all right if I call you that here," Lady Hardin began. "Tell us about your horses. When we move you ladies over to the townhouse, we don't want to leave your pets."

"I ride my horse, Sable, almost every day before the rest of the household rises," Elizabeth said. "Now that my stepbrother has returned, I worry he will see she's mine and something could happen. I do not know him for his gentle nature," she said diplomatically.

"I confess, I surprised my mother by having agreed with her suggestion to move you both, but as I devolved a couple of issues, I realized you'd be safer if I could ensure you were being cared for, and since my mother had already shown she was in favor it, I decided to go ahead with it," Alan said.

"Thank goodness you said that! I thought I had missed a step in my age," his mother said, sipping her cup of tea.

Jeremy barked with laughter. "I caught Mother's look, but she pulled it off beautifully. We will be happy to have such lovely ladies as part of our household. We have a very large townhouse that needs to be filled with people."

"You are so right, son," his mother agreed.

"I'm thrilled to move in with you, even though I shall miss my bedroom," Penny chimed in. "I have already packed all the things I don't want to leave and shoved them under my bed," she added thoughtfully.

"Who accompanies you on your rides to Hyde Park, Miss Elizabeth?" Alan asked.

"Elizabeth, please. And Joe, our ostler, always gets a footman, usually Ross, to ride behind me and ensure my safety."

"Good. Well, it would be my pleasure to do so tomorrow morning, if you are interested," Alan said.

He didn't miss the arched brows of his brother and mother. But he needed to see what his ward did in the morning—virtually alone, but for one footman. At least that was what he was telling himself.

"I would be happy for you to join us, Lord Halsburg," Elizabeth said.

Alan nodded. "Then, it's settled. What time do you go?" He couldn't account for the pleasure that shot through him when she agreed.

"Seven in the morning. I'm usually back and changed before our stepmother breaks her fast," Elizabeth replied.

"I will be there," he replied. "Does your maid ride?"

"Goodness, no! That's largely why I take the footman. I enjoy riding and Sable needs the exercise. It gives me time alone before I face whatever the day brings," Elizabeth said, smiling.

Alan smiled, feeling lighter than he had in weeks, certain it was because he was getting a better grasp on his guardianship and its responsibilities. It was the efficacious smile on his mother's face and the expressive one on his sibling's face that gave him pause—but he would not let their teasing mar his achievement as a guardian.

# CHAPTER 8

FOUR DAYS LATER

*E*lizabeth held Sable's face in her hands, nuzzling her between the eyes and nuzzling her velvety nose. "I'm looking forward to today's ride, Sable," she whispered, before mounting the horse for her morning ride. The horse had been given to her by her father and, outside of her sister, was the most important thing in her life, and she loved both dearly. Riding was something she looked forward to doing, but having the earl accompany her made it more fun. For the last three mornings, they had ridden through Hyde Park, followed by chocolate or hot tea at Gunter's, at the end of their morning ride.

The two laughed and talked about anything—normally mundane things that, when talked about with him, seemed interesting. Since she and Penny had moved into the Halsburg house, things seemed calmer. She no longer allowed herself to think about Daniel walking up behind her and cornering her in a room, as he had been fond of doing.

The park was empty at this time of year, as most of the gentry had moved back to their country homes. The horses were on a slow trot as they passed through the main entrance to the park.

"Do you have a preference on which path to take?" Alan asked, jolting her from her musings.

"No," she said. "It's your choice today."

"Wonderful. I thought we could try a different path," he said, turning to ensure his footman was following them. "James doesn't seem to mind this early assignment."

"Ross told me he spoke to James to acquaint him with my riding habits." A snort escaped, and she bit her lower lip to control her laughter.

"What habits would *those* be?" he asked, raising a brow.

"Mmm. I've been known to take off and race Sable across the fields —that sort of thing."

He grew serious. "I know you were fond of your footman and hated to leave the staff you'd known for years. Perhaps opportunities to increase staff will present themselves along the way, particularly when we return to the manor house. We hired your maid and Penny's governess and to do more would give the baroness a reason to cry foul."

"I understood. But they will watch out for each other. Walters runs a tight ship."

"Yes, I got that impression." He moved his horse closer. "You and your sister seem to have transitioned smoothly into Halsburg House. I hope you are finding everything to your liking."

"Oh yes, my lord! My room is almost like the one my mama decorated for me. And the cheerful colors of the nursery meet my sister's approval."

He smiled. "I understand from Mother that you had a secret hiding spot. Hidey spots, as I called them, are important. Please tell Penny that she should create her own—and I do not require knowing the location."

She realized he knew about her conversation with Lady Hardin. It was no matter. She had grown tired of feeling confined to the house to protect her very basic belongings from being vandalized. When her stepmother allowed her son to move home, Elizabeth's stress doubled. "You and your mother have made us so comfortable. I never imagined leaving my home, but you both have been most welcoming. Except for Lady Rollins' demands for compensation for Sable and Jane, I hope our moving created no other problems."

"Everything worked out," he said, holding her gaze. "I settled a nominal amount on Sable, which was fair, and Lady Rollins backed off her demand for Jane. That was utter ridiculousness."

Elizabeth remained perplexed as to why her rich stepmother had become so money-grabbing. *Papa was an extremely wealthy man*, she thought, looking away. "What happened to his money?"

"I don't know, but surely something will come to light," the earl returned.

Her face heated when she realized she had spoken a thought out loud. "I hadn't meant to say that. However, she made us live as if we were at the door to poverty—something I cannot understand."

"I have wondered the same. It seems counter to her ostentatious personality. But let us not allow her on our ride this morning."

Elizabeth's horse followed his horse's lead, and they veered left onto the path that snaked alongside the river. For a few minutes, both settled into a pensive quietness. "I like this scenery. When I ride by myself—I mean with Ross behind me—I stay on the main trails. This is more wooded—it's nice."

"Shall we make our morning stop for chocolate at Gunter's?" he asked, with a smile curling at his mouth.

Her heart gave a twist as she took in his handsome face. *I'm really attracted to this man.* Ignoring common sense and cutting their ride short, she nodded. "Yes, please. I'm chilly."

A few minutes later, they sat in their usual spot by the fireplace. His footman had Sable and Maximillian, the earl's horse, as well as his own, in a small stable near the parlor. The earl also made certain James received a hot cup of chocolate. Secretly, Elizabeth thought the sticky buns and chocolate were the real reason for James' happiness with this morning's assignment.

"I wonder if you would honor me by calling me by my given name —Alan—when we are not around others," he said, abruptly setting his teacup on the table and looking into her eyes. His gloved hand slid slowly across the table and covered her own.

Delicious pulses of energy shot up her arm, a feeling she noticed each time he grew close, and she savored the comfort it gave her. Propriety told her to move her hand, but her heart wouldn't let her. She enjoyed the time spent with this man and woke up looking forward to seeing both him and Sable.

A nerve quickened in her throat. "What about my being your ward?" *This was what I wanted to do, isn't it? I could have opted not to go to Gunter's,* she reminded herself. "Won't people think it odd to hear me call you by your given name?"

"If you mean my family or staff—you will find them to be accepting. You would still address me formally in front of company. I suppose some might. But you will be twenty-one in a few months," he offered. "January, correct? I've been thinking it's a few months, but it's only one."

She grinned. "And do you keep up with everyone in the household's birthdays?"

"Only those important to me," he said meaningfully. "Generally, Mother reminds me of the important ones. But with yours, I've had lots of reason to become more acquainted."

His eyes held hers.

"I looked over some paperwork yesterday that had you and your sister's birthdays. Penny's is in April. Yours is January the fifth. I kept thinking it was a few months away—I suppose because when I assumed the guardianship, there was so much to take in, I glossed over some things."

He gently squeezed her hand. "Care to take a walk? The horses will be fine with James. I promise," Alan said.

She nodded. She loved his company. *How did I not see the person he was when I met him a year ago? I didn't see the man he is.*

"Good," he said. "I'll be right back." He spoke with one of the staff and they pointed to a young boy waiting outside the door. The boy immediately came into the shop. Elizabeth noticed he was missing several of his front teeth, and his clothes were too small for him, pulling in all directions to cover his small, lithe body.

"M'name's Robbie, guvnor," she heard him say.

The conversation between the two of them warmed her.

She saw Alan withdraw a coin and tuck it in Robbie's hand before handing him a small tray of food and drink. "Take this note and this warm food to the man in the stable who is holding our horses. His name is James. Tell him we are delayed but plan to leave shortly. The coin and the second bun are for you."

The boy opened his hand and looked back at Alan, his face splitting into a grin. "A crown! Oh, thank ye, milord. Thank ye! I can surely afford a good doctor for m'mum."

Alan walked back to the table.

Elizabeth wanted to say something like *that was really nice,* but stayed silent.

"Care to take a short walk? There's a place I'd like to show you." Alan held out his arm and Elizabeth took it. "We will stay in the public view, so I won't compromise your reputation." A few minutes later, they were at a small spot on the Serpentine. "I used to come here and fish when I was a boy. My father brought me. It's the most private spot I know in the park, and it's out in the open. I occasionally come and relive memories of my father," he said. "Let's sit."

Her heart fluttered wildly as he took her hand. "Only if you promise I won't fall in." He showed a log that sat a foot from the water's edge and helped her sit, then joined her.

"This is pretty and very quiet. I used to fish with my father," she said. "When he didn't have a son, he taught me to ride a horse, fish, and shoot an arrow."

"You enjoy archery? I would have never guessed," he said, sounding disbelieving.

"I do. The last time I shot was with my father. We were teaching Penny," she said. Her throat caught at the memory.

"I haven't used arrows since before I left for war, so I'm rather rusty."

She noticed he edged closer. "I had forgotten you fought in the war," she whispered.

Elizabeth watched him looking around. "We are alone, Elizabeth. I realize I'm your guardian and you are my ward. When you are near, I can think of little but wanting to kiss you." He cupped her face. "I'd like to kiss you now."

A knot formed in her stomach. She wanted the kiss as much as he did, but this didn't seem like the right time. There was a tree next to her, which provided some coverage.

"My lo . . . Alan. I don't think this is a good idea. Not . . . not that I don't want your kiss. I do," she hastily added. "Goodness, help me, but I want to kiss you. But if someone sees us, it could cause problems for you, Alan, for both of us."

"We are alone at this hour . . . in this place," he murmured, moving closer. "I see no one, but your concerns are valid. Yet, my heart tells me to take the risk," he said, leaning towards her.

"Do you trust me?" he whispered.

She wanted to answer, but could only nod, with her attention firmly on his mouth moving towards hers.

A soft gust of wind rustled through the near-empty limbs of the trees surrounding them, forcing the remaining leaves from the branches to waft through the air onto the serene waters of the Serpentine. The scene seemed like something out of a book, she thought, taking it all in as his face inclined towards hers. He placed his lips on hers and she closed her eyes, relishing the warmth and soft-ness of his lips, wanting more.

She parted her lips as his increased their pressure, and his tongue explored the recesses of her mouth. Elizabeth tasted him, the sweet-ness of the honeyed bun they had shared, mixed with the lemony tart-ness of his hot tea—both tastes melding with the chocolate that had lingered on her tongue. She felt as if she were tasting the vestiges of a secret aphrodisiac.

His face moved slightly, and his hands framed hers as he sought more of her, deepening his taste. Tremors of sensation rushed through her body, and she clung to him, twinning her hands in the hair at his nape. When he slowed his movements, she tugged him closer, reacting to a surge of need she had never experienced before. *She felt wanton but wanted.*

Time stood still while they kissed, tongues meeting, probing, searching, and caressing, until he pulled back and broke off the kiss. Elizabeth's energy felt depleted, and she momentarily felt limp—but strangely feeling renewed. Summoning her reserve of energy, she drew back and opened her eyes, staring into his.

"I will never regret taking that kiss," he whispered.

"Me either," she said, still slightly dazed.

Slowly, he helped her stand. "We should get back," Alan said, squeezing her hand. "Riding with you in the morning is a habit I could get used to."

"I could do it every day of my life," she whispered to herself.

As they walked back to Gunter's, they spotted James holding the reins of the horses and laughing with Robbie.

When he saw them, the boy stepped forward. "Yer back, guvnor! Ye may wonder why I'm still here with your man."

"I'm glad to meet you, Robbie," Elizabeth said.

"Pleased to make your acquaintance, your ladyship," Robbie said, smoothly taking Elizabeth's gloved hand and kissing it.

He turned to Alan. "M'mum is sick with a cough and needs a doctor. I'd be pleased if ye had some work fer me." A short-legged black dog barked from behind him and moseyed up alongside him.

"This 'ere's Trina," he said, patting her head. "Would it be all right if she followed me to yer place? I always split my food and water with her. She was starving when I found her, but we've become friends and I keep her with me as much as possible. As you can see, she lies low while I work." His voice took on a note of self-importance at his accomplishment.

Alan glanced at a smiling Elizabeth. "I think we can find something for you to do. Bring Trina. James will introduce you to my stable manager. He will find work for you and my cook can rustle up some food for your friend there."

"Thank you, guvnor!"

Elizabeth's heart somersaulted. The man was the epitome of kindness. He had been nothing but helpful and honest with her. Knowing she would spend Christmastide with his family seemed like a miracle.

Alan glanced at Robbie and then at his footman. "James, see you make the introduction," he said, giving a knowing nod.

"Yes, my lord," the footman said, hoisting the boy behind him.

"We should get back," Elizabeth said, amazed at the transaction she had just witnessed. Alan had the biggest heart. "I imagine his mother has consumption," she said, shuddering.

"Poor lad. You are probably right. I'll speak with Mother and see if she has any ideas."

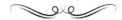

ALAN GLANCED AT ELIZABETH, who leaned forward and whispered to Sable. The content expression on her face pleased him. He had never kept a mistress, but there had been other women in his life. Yet, this woman was different. Never had he felt such an intense attraction. And never had he experienced such a kiss as he had experienced with Elizabeth. *I care for her.* His heart had never been engaged to any woman, but he feared Elizabeth Rollins owned a healthy portion of it.

Over the week, they had shared countless hours of laughing and telling stories of their lives. The attraction to her overwhelmed him to where he could no longer deny himself.

"Was it your first . . . kiss?" he asked.

She looked at him, her eyes veiled by her thick black lashes. "There have been others that have given me what they called a kiss, but I could not put their efforts in the same category as what I experienced with you, my lord."

"Alan," he reminded her.

She maintained her focus ahead. "I'm sorry. Alan," she whispered loud enough for his ears, alone. "No other kiss could equal that."

"Shall we ride tomorrow morning?" he asked. "I promise to keep it to the ride and perhaps, our stop at Gunter's. Nothing further."

"Yes, I enjoy our mornings," she replied.

They heard hooves coming up fast from behind. It was James and Robbie.

"My lord," James said, a bit out of breath as he pulled alongside Alan's horse. "I could not see his face, but Robbie was the first to notice a man following us. He said he saw the man at Gunter's while watching the horses with me, but until he saw him trailing us, he thought nothing of it. The man keeps a steady distance, hanging well behind us. I looked behind, pretending to be speaking with Robbie, and I saw him move to the side of the road, hiding. That happened twice."

"Let us get Miss Elizabeth home safely. How fast can the dog run, do you think?"

"She has short legs, so I think not fast," James replied.

"We are almost at the townhouse. We need to get Miss Rollins back safely." He turned to Elizabeth. "Please go into the house as soon as we pull into the drive. I will take Sable to the stable." He needed to check on the footmen he had hired.

"Whom could it be?" she asked. One name immediately popped into her head. *Surely not,* she reasoned. "Be careful."

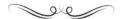

A TALL MAN stepped from a dark corner behind a stable, a house away from the mansion the earl called his *townhouse*. He watched the earl and his footman walk the horses into the stable. A large brown overcoat and a slouchy brown hat hid his face, blending him into the scenery.

Watching Halsburg speak to his guards made him laugh to himself. Today hadn't worked out the way he had planned, but there was always tomorrow. "You think you can outwit me, Lord Halsburg, but I'm determined. You will learn I mean business," he said, narrowing his eyes. Mounting the tall, black horse standing behind him, he kept to the shaded side of the street, replaying what he had witnessed earlier in the park, fueling his anger.

# CHAPTER 9

"These are for me?" Robbie asked, putting the pitchfork down. "I've been putting fresh straw in the stalls. I ain't n'er had a real job before—unless you count climbing into a chimney. But that was when I was smaller."

Elizabeth's heart twisted. This child had been on his own for too long. Alan had already sent a doctor to see his mother today. *I hope they can help her. Losing a mother is so hard and he's doing his best to care for her.* Turning her attention to Robbie, she passed him two pairs of breeches Jane had made for him. "Jane made these for you. We hope you like them." Her maid had taken some older pants belonging to the late earl and made them into smaller pants for Robbie. It had been Alan's idea.

"I've never had new clothes in my life," he said, threatening tears.

"You do now, Robbie. With winter here, his lordship thought you needed a few things," Elizabeth said. The late earl's clothing had given Jane plenty of material to make the child's pants. Elizabeth reached into a small box and withdrew a grey and black plaid jacket. "This used to be my father's favorite jacket when he was outdoors. I thought it might be perfect to resize for you."

"Ain't n'er had a new coat, Miss Elizabeth," he said, wiping a tear. "I figure it was my lucky day when his lordship asked me to watch yer horses. Now I got me a job and a way to help m'mum."

Elizabeth pulled him close and hugged him before pointing to Jane. "My sweet maid, Jane, did a good job guessing your size based on her observations. We wanted it to be a surprise, so we couldn't measure you properly." Reaching into her bag, Elizabeth pulled out another item made from the plaid coat. "This is a pelisse for Trina."

"I n'er heard of a coat fer a dog, but that don't matter. She gets cold and burrows into the straw at night to get warm, but running around during the day makes her cold," Robbie explained. He whistled, and they heard the dog dig herself out of the straw in the stall next to them.

"That dog is hilarious. Come here, girl," Elizabeth said, stooping down and scratching behind Trina's ear. Taking the doggie pelisse, she slipped Trina's head through the neck opening before adjusting it around the girth of the pet, cinching it with small fabric hooks. Before Elizabeth could stand, Trina licked her on the chin, eliciting a giggle. "You should be warm now, girl."

"She likes it," Robbie said.

"Jane and I must head to town."

Robbie stood up. "James plans to go with you, right?" Robbie asked.

"I think so. I'm not sure who is going. But I'm certain his stable manager has it well in hand. Lady Hardin feels we need one more item in the boxing baskets and I volunteered to go."

"I ain't n'er seen a boxing basket," Robbie said, slowly scratching his chin.

Elizabeth smiled. "I'd explain it to you, but the carriage is being brought around, so I must leave. Lord Halsburg wanted you to have these clothes as soon as possible. However, I promise you will learn what *boxing baskets* are."

ROBBIE FOLLOWED Miss Elizabeth and watched James assist her and the maid into the coach. When it lurched forward, he saw the driver. The two times he had seen the earl's driver take the coach, the man had worn a taller hat. The man driving Miss Elizabeth's coach wore one that covered half his face. He had never seen him before, and Robbie had met everyone in the stables.

Robbie ran over to James. "Weren't you supposed to go?"

"I was," James said, looking puzzled. "It pulled off as soon as I shut the door."

"Get the earl," Robbie said. "A bad man just took Miss Elizabeth."

Running as hard as he could, Robbie chased the coach as it turned down streets haphazardly through Mayfair, but traffic soon blocked his vision, and he lost sight of it. *Something was wrong—he just knew it!* Desperate to help Miss Elizabeth, he turned and ran back to find the earl.

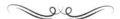

"WE SHOULD TALK. I left *En Garde*," Jeremy said, entering Alan's study and shutting the door. His brother walked to one of the leather chairs in front of the desk and sat down.

"What's going on, Jeremy?" Alan asked, looking up from his ledgers.

"Remember the man we had seen with Chadwick the day we met with Nelson and Shefford? I found him."

"Where?" Alan asked, picking up two clean glasses.

Jeremy held up his hand. "No brandy. This could be serious. Remember when we were leaving the club the other day and we saw Chadwick handing a man something?"

Alan nodded.

"I saw the same man today and followed him. He ducked into a tavern near the fencing club, and Jonathan and I followed him. The man told us Chadwick had tried to hire him for a job, but word on the street was, Chadwick's credit was no longer good—so, he refused him.

"And?"

"He said Chadwick mumbled something about taking back what should have been his."

"What the devil does that mean?" Alan said, easing back as the feeling of foreboding crept over him. "I'm expecting Ruben any minute. When he comes, you're welcome to stay."

Travers tapped on the door and showed Ruben into the study.

"We were just talking about you," Alan said.

"Good things, I hope. Good morning, Lord Halsburg, Mr. Hardin," the older man said in a grim tone. "I have the information you wanted. There's a lot to unpack."

"Please, sit down. Can I offer you a hot cup of tea, anything?" Alan said. Hair pricked his neck. Something felt wrong.

"I'd love a cup," Ruben said.

Alan nodded to Travers, who went to the kitchen for the tea.

"It's been unusually cold today, especially with the wind." Ruben took a seat and withdrew a paper from his vest pocket. His eyebrows drew together in a frown as he stared at it. Finally, he said, "I did an investigation on Mr. Daniel Chadwick for Mr. Nelson's fencing club and what we found was not the best news, my lord. Mr. Nelson asked that I share it with you immediately. Let me start with what we know."

Ruben's slow pace of divulging information made Alan fidgety. He fought the impulse to snap and ask him to hurry up and tell them. *Ruben's doing me the favor*, he reminded himself. Instead, he chewed the inside of his lip, a bad habit of his when stressed, and allowed the man to plod along.

Steepling his fingers, Ruben leaned back in the chair. "It seems Mr. Chadwick came into a bit of money following the death of his stepfather, Lord Rollins . . . but that was not Lord Rollins' wish. Chadwick has a small allowance, not one that supports his current habits around town. One of the bank tellers at the bank where your uncle did, and I believe you, as well, Lord Halsburg, do business—found himself in a bit of financial difficulty with Chadwick. To gain his way free, the teller agreed to alter some of the bank records.

"Of course, the man has been arrested now," Rubens continued. "And what's gone is gone, as the saying goes, but oddly, it was the widow's finances he altered. *His mother!* Can you believe that?"

Alan grimaced as he attempted to hold his control. Instead of saying anything, he shook his head.

"Yes, well," Ruben went on. "It was Chadwick's mother whose actions led to this discovery. And to the teller's arrest. She has been complaining that something is not right with her income from her husband's estate and finally, she complained to the chairman of the bank, who launched a quiet investigation. As your uncle had already taken over the other two-thirds of the estate designated for his daughters, those monies were safe and untouchable.

"The magistrate and our men have been looking for Chadwick today, but as of the time I arrived here, we have not found out his whereabouts and he is unaware the magistrate wants him. Curiously, the arrested man assured me in my discussions with him that Chadwick only asked him to alter his mother's account and divert regular payments to him. According to the man, Chadwick said he was employing other methods to access his stepsisters' inheritance." He took a relaxing breath. "This is the latest news—and of course, isn't even known to Mr. Nelson. But since you are the guardian, I felt it was your business to know everything."

"That accounts for why she diverted the funds I sent for the wards' use," Alan said, thinking out loud.

"Yes. It would," Jeremy agreed. "Still, it doesn't make it right."

"Is there anything else I should know?" Alan demanded.

"There is more. Chadwick has had several more complaints made against him in recent years. There were two complaints about drunken abuse against the daughter of a London merchant, but they dropped the charges. To protect his daughter, the merchant refused to talk about it. The merchant told me he had threatened both him and his daughter," Ruben said.

"There were also unsubstantiated rumors of his involvement in a riding accident—the saddle was tampered with."

Alan looked at Jeremy. "What did they determine?"

"The only witness died, and the suspicions died with them. Nothing was investigated further. If anyone looked for a conviction or court document against the man, they wouldn't find one. But we found people willing to talk. And I believe that where there is smoke, there is fire. The man stole from his mother!"

"It explains a lot. He allowed his mother to move him into the house, where he could find out more about the girls' inheritance." Alan's temper rose.

"I plan to pursue all three situations—rumors and all," Ruben said. "Allegations or suspicions were dropped, and nothing was pursued. I shared the last two incidents with Nelson; Chadwick didn't meet his club's character standards and he turned his membership down. He said the man left his club, furious. But Nelson and his brother are experts with swords and guns. Sagely, Chadwick chose not to test his luck."

The door to the study burst open and Robbie ran inside. "My lord, I think Miss Elizabeth is gone," he said, struggling to catch his breath. "I tried to catch 'em, but I lost sight of the carriage."

All three men rose. "What do you mean . . . *gone?*" Alan demanded, standing with such fervor, he nearly turned over his desk.

"A man took her with yer carriage. She and her maid, Miss Jane, said they needed stuff for the boxing things. When the carriage pulled away, I saw the driver looked different than I'd seen afore. I couldn't see his face 'cause of his hat . . . like the other day with the man following us from the park. I ain't been here long, guvnor, but yer driver has a different hat." The boy leaned over to catch his breath.

James appeared behind him at the door. "He's right, my lord. They've taken her. There was a footman on the back wearing your livery—but you had hired a few new ones this past week, and I didn't pay enough attention. I found the driver nursing his head in the back of the barn with his clothes missing."

"I suspect you will find a footman somewhere missing his livery and nursing injuries, as well," Ruben said. He turned to Alan. "We will find her, Lord Halsburg. Mark my words."

Alan's heart lodged in his throat. *He had to find her.* "We have to find them before something happens."

Lady Hardin rushed into the room. "I heard you in my parlor. What has happened to Elizabeth?"

"She's been taken. We must find her, Mother. I believe he took her."

"Who is *he?*" Ruben asked.

"Chadwick," Alan and his mother said, together.

"I have men. We will comb the town and investigate every place he has lived or been seen," Ruben said.

"Jeremy, we've got to find her," Alan said.

"What about her maid, Jane? They were both going into town," his mother said.

"Robbie thinks someone highjacked the carriage once the ladies got into it."

*My heart is in that carriage,* Alan realized. All kinds of scenarios played out in his head, but only one name resonated. *Daniel Chadwick.* She had always been frightened of the man.

# CHAPTER 10

*omething was wrong.* When Elizabeth looked out the window as the carriage lurched forward, she saw it leave James behind, and James usually accompanied her to town. Alan's driver, Mr. Pickett, drove more steadily than this—at least when Lady Hardin or Alan was in the carriage.

The carriage flew through the streets of Mayfair and took curves on two wheels, tossing its white-knuckled occupants from the left side of the carriage to the right. Jane's eyes were as big as saucers as she and Elizabeth fought against motion sickness, holding on for their lives.

"Something's very wrong, miss," Jane said when the carriage turned off the main road. "I don't mind telling you, I'm scared."

"Me too," Elizabeth admitted. The carriage stopped, and the door jerked open. An unshaven, foul-smelling man stood there.

"Ladies, you need to get out." When they didn't move, he pulled a small gun from his pocket. "Git. Out." He motioned with the gun. "Carl here will escort you."

A man in a Halsburg livery stepped up behind them, slapping the toothy man on the back of the head. "Don't you know not to say our names? Now, you've probably messed up the job!"

"They won't get out," the toothy man complained, dangerously wielding the gun.

"Did you tell them you'd shoot them, stupid?" the liveried man asked.

"I did. And don't call me *stupid*. Where's the bloody boss? *He* can do it himself," the toothy one snarled. "It's his job. He promised me this carriage and I need to move it to the docks before the ship leaves."

"Hey, I get half. Don't forget the horses. They're worth sum'fin'," Carl said.

"Why are you men doing this?" Elizabeth demanded, cutting into their argument. "You mentioned *he*. Who is *he*?"

"*He* would be me." She recognized that voice. "Daniel, why are you doing this?"

"Money," he said simply. "I don't know what you're worth, but I suspect a lot—as my wife." He snatched the gun from the toothy man and shoved him. "Give me that! Plans have changed. We are taking this carriage to Gretna Green. It has no markings on it, and people won't know who it belongs to. Now." He pointed to Jane. "You. Out of the carriage. The extra baggage will slow us down."

"You are not leaving her in the middle of nowhere," Elizabeth cried.

"Shut up!" he warned. "Out." His focus was on Jane, who, trembling, picked up her skirts and exited the carriage. "Tie her up."

"But boss, she's seen our faces," the one named Carl whined.

"Do it! She also knows our names," but there's nothing anyone can do. Tie her up and put her in the dark stable over there."

Elizabeth looked around and realized she was in the mews somewhere in Mayfair. No wonder the carriage kept turning. They were circling the town. "Don't hurt Jane," she cried. When he turned back to face her, Daniel wore a wicked smile. Pulling his arm from behind his back, he grabbed her and held a cloth over her nose and mouth.

"I don't plan to struggle with you the whole trip. When you are my wife, you will learn your place," he said ominously, pinching her on the breast.

Elizabeth struggled as hard as she could against him, but the world grew darker. She heard voices, but they sounded further and further away until, after what seemed like an eternity, she slipped into the dark void.

ALAN AND JEREMY rushed up the steps to the Rollins' household and banged on the door until Walters opened the door. "We need to see Lady Rollins," he demanded. "*And her son.*"

"Mr. Chadwick hasn't been seen here in several days . . . except for a visit earlier today," Walters said.

"Then, take me to Lady Rollins . . . immediately," Alan insisted, ready to push past the butler if need be. Instead, Walters stepped aside. "Is everything all right with Miss Elizabeth and Miss Penny?"

"That's why we've come. Miss Elizabeth has been taken and we think Chadwick did it."

The older man gasped. "Oh, Lord! Come in. Follow me to the parlor," he said, leading Alan and Jeremy.

The retainer opened the door only to see Lady Rollins trussed up and gagged, rolling on the carpeted floor.

"Gawd! What happened here? Are you all right, my lady?" Walters asked as Alan ripped the gag off the baroness.

"Did Chadwick do this?" Jeremy asked.

"He did," the baroness whimpered. "He demanded my jewelry. When I refused, he tied me up, ripped off my earrings and rings, and tore up the room, looking for my safety. He didn't find it. I'm shocked no one heard him. I've been laying on the floor for hours." As if their presence suddenly dawned on her, she looked up. "Why are you men here?"

"He kidnapped Elizabeth," Alan said, helping her up.

Lady Rollins gasped. "What? Oh no!"

"You brought him into this house with two vulnerable young women, and everyone in the *ton* knows his reputation—what he did to that scullery maid, and why he was made to leave." Alan's eyes blazed and he leaned into her ear. "Trust me, I know what you have been doing, but will keep it to myself unless you refuse to help."

Ross walked into the room. "My lord, Lady Rollins. Did I hear someone say Mr. Chadwick has taken Miss Elizabeth? I saw him leave earlier and head into the mews. He was on foot."

"There! You are wrong about my son," Lady Rollins charged weakly. "He couldn't have done it.'"

"Even you know that's a lie. He had her kidnapped from my stable area on the mews. Where did he go, Ross?"

"I was so curious, I followed him," the footman replied. "He hasn't returned here in days —until today. I wondered if he was staying somewhere." He looked penitently in Lady Rollins' direction.

"Don't apologize. If he has done this, and I suspect there is more, the man is a criminal," Alan said.

"How dare . . ." Lady Rollins started.

"*You* most of all know what your son can do. Tell me what you know, or I will pull my bills for my wards and speak to every one of the vendors. Stealing is a crime, and I have friends in high places," Alan threatened.

She looked away. "He has it in his head to marry her. I tried to direct him to other ladies, like Lady Rose Gunter. But he has nothing to offer a lady—no title, no wealth. I just realized he's been into my accounts and spending my money all over town." She slumped onto the couch. I'm so sorry," she said, holding her face in her hands. "I must ask your forgiveness."

"I won't have any forgiveness if one hair on Elizabeth's head is harmed," Alan said. "Let's go, Jeremy, Ross." The men started out the door.

"I'm coming, too. The girl has been like a granddaughter to me all her life," Walters said. "I promised her father years ago I would watch out for her."

The door slammed behind them, and the four men took off down the steps. Jeremy and Alan mounted their horses and followed behind Walters and Ross to the stable, where both men got horses. The small group followed the mews road that ran behind the Rollins' house.

"It's very close," Ross said as they approached an intersection.

When they turned onto the street running behind his family's mansion, they heard barking and a boy's voice.

"What are Robbie and Trina doing here?" Alan asked. The dog was furiously sniffing the ground near a much smaller townhouse with a stable behind it. Everything was dark inside the house. It was obvious the owners had relocated to the country.

"The boy and his dog found the stable I saw Chadwick enter earlier," Ross said, opening an unlocked door and lighting the lamp inside.

Muffled sounds of a woman drew their attention to a stall to their right and the sight of Jane trussed up and gagged.

"Oh, my God!" Walters bellowed, sliding from his horse. "Jane." The older man bent down and ripped the bindings from her hands and face and held her against his shoulder while she cried with relief.

"He's taken her. I saw him put something over her face and drug her. Then, he said he planned to marry her. It couldn't have been more than an hour. They have your unmarked coach, my lord," Jane said raggedly. "I could have been here forever, and no one would have known it. Thank goodness you found me."

"You have these three to thank, Jeremy said, pointing to Robbie, Trina, and Ross. If not for them, we may never have found you."

"Gretna Green, I'm guessing," Alan said angrily. "I should have foreseen this. I will leave you with Ross and Walters, Jane."

Jane gave a small nod.

"Jeremy, we need to go," Alan urged.

"I'd like to help, too, my lord," Ross said. "That is if you can use an extra hand."

"Ross, I need you to get the magistrate. You and Walters need to make sure you tell everything you heard Lady Rollins say, and make sure they interview Jane. That would be a big help."

"Thank you, my lord. I will take care of it," Ross said. "We will take care of Jane."

"Thank you," Alan said.

Alan and his brother stopped at their townhouse and asked a

waiting groom to hold their horses. They met Nelson as they ran to the house.

"Your mother sent Everly to find me, and he let me know what had happened. I'm here to help," Jonathan explained.

"We need to get weapons and leave," Alan said, opening his gun cabinet, they chose guns, and he and his brother grabbed their swords and overcoats.

"Be careful, all of you," his mother said, as she walked into the study. "The man is unhinged. Take extra care."

"We promise, Mother," Alan said. "I have no intention of losing anything to this madman. I must find her before he hurts her." Despite his best efforts, his eyes misted.

His mother hugged him. "You love her," she whispered.

He nodded.

"You will get there in time, Alan. Elizabeth is a fighter."

"From your lips to God's ears, Mother," Jeremy said. "We will watch out for each other."

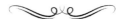

ELIZABETH AWOKE BUT LAY STILL. Keeping her eyes shielded by her dark lashes, she tried to see and feel around her. Her legs and hands were tied, but she refused to panic. Thankfully, there was still daylight. Daniel sat across from her and looked to be sleeping. But it would be just like Daniel to trick her, so she kept her eyes as near to closed as she could.

The last thing she wanted was a confrontation with him. Silently praying Alan would rescue her. *But how would he know she was gone?* Unless someone discovered the driver and footman in the barn, she didn't see the likelihood. She and Jane were supposed to be in town, so no one might know she was gone. Elizabeth tried but couldn't recognize anything from the surrounding scenery.

She shuddered. He planned to marry her, and that would mean days in this cramped carriage with him.

Doing her best to control her breathing, she rested and remained still.

Abruptly, the coach turned the corner, and it sounded as if something fell off the coach from beneath the cab. Startled, she sat up.

"Ah! You are awake," Daniel said, sitting up. I'm sorry to have to do this to you, Elizabeth, but you will pay for what your father did."

"And that was?" she asked.

"He left me nothing in his will," he said. "And to make matters worse, he took away much of my allowance."

*He owed you nothing. You are a horrible person,* she thought to herself. Daniel was crazy and mean. She realized that he had sat up because she had. *He didn't hear the problem beneath the carriage.* As frightened as she was, she would not think about being injured in a carriage accident. If that helped her escape from this madman, so be it.

"Later, we will stop for the night. I will introduce you as my wife," Daniel said. "I will decide on the last name soon. It could be fun."

"I will never be your wife," she spat. "Remember . . . you will have to sleep sometime."

"Ha! I see some of my mother's wit has rubbed off on you. Believe me . . . you will be a wife to me. It is important in my revenge against your father." He withdrew a pocketknife and casually cleaned his fingernails.

*Disgusting man,* she thought.

The carriage took a corner too quickly, throwing her into Daniel, and he pulled her close. Without the ability to move her hands, she could do little to free herself. The more she struggled, the tighter he held her.

"This is a surprise," he taunted. His breath stank with the smell of stale whiskey.

"Unhand me, you lecher," she demanded.

"You still wear jasmine," he said, breathing her hair. "It became my favorite scent years ago." He leaned down and nibbled her ear, tracing down her neck, lightly kissing her cheek. Turning sharply, she found his ear and bit as hard as she could, drawing blood.

"You bitch!" he said, drawing his hand until he stopped midair.

"Are you going to hit me?" she taunted. "If you despoil me, you had better sleep with one eye open," she seethed. Fear had deserted her and all she felt was fury. His face reddened with rage. *Perhaps that wasn't my best move.*

He said nothing for a long moment. "There's an inn up ahead and we will stay long enough for sustenance. There is much of the day to go. I will untie you, but you had better act the part of a loving wife."

A grinding noise sounded from beneath the carriage and grew much louder. She noted the concern in his eyes. "We may not make it to the inn," she said heatedly. "Your stooges have almost broken this carriage with their horrible driving."

"Shut up, or I will forget about any kindness I might have towards you," he seethed.

Shortly, the carriage turned off the main road, slowing down to a stop in the gravel drive of an inn.

Daniel reached into his pocket and withdrew the knife, freeing the bindings on her hands and feet.

They walked into the inn together with the point of his knife in her back, reminding her he was in charge. It was dark, and as her eyes adjusted, she recognized Alan and Jeremy sitting at a table in a far corner, both wearing hats. Alan met her eyes and shook his head. "Shall we sit over here?" she asked, indicating something on the far side of the room. She glanced again in Alan's direction, they were gone.

"Take that table," Daniel said. "I want to be able to see the room."

She did as she was told and sat down, relieved to have the knife out of her back.

"You were right, brother," a familiar baritone voice said, approaching behind Daniel. "This was a perfect watering hole—you knew he couldn't resist."

"'Tis a well-known place to assuage one's thirst. By now, his flunkies have been secured," Jeremy said.

"You're too late, Halsburg. She threw herself at me earlier, and I obliged her needs," Daniel hissed. "We will be married."

Alan fought to maintain control. "No, you won't," he said, leaning over and whispering loudly. "You are going to make this easy." He jerked Chadwick's arm and helped him to his feet.

"You won't get away with this. I will make you pay," Chadwick claimed.

"I think not. It's you that won't get away with this," Jeremy said, taking his other arm. "The king's agents met us on our way out of town, and they are here to take you back to London."

John Ruben stepped from the corner of the room with one of his men. "The king has expressed a serious interest in meeting with you. There is the matter of a carriage accident he especially wishes to discuss. We will have much to discuss." Two of the king's men jerked Daniel's arm behind his back and removed him from the table. Away from Elizabeth.

"May I have a moment?" Elizabeth asked, stepping back from Alan. "I have something I want to say to Daniel."

Alan looked at her. "Are you sure?"

"Very," she said, walking to where her stepbrother stood secured by the king's men and sneering in her direction. "This is for you, Daniel." She drew back her hand and a crack sounded, as she slapped her stepbrother as hard as she could manage across his face.

Alan gently took her hand and pulled her away. "Thank you for your help, Mr. Ruben. You can take him away." Alan pulled Elizabeth close. "He will never come near you again," he whispered, seeking her lips and covering them with his own. "It terrified me when I realized you had been taken, my sweet Elizabeth."

"I kept looking for you. And you came for me," she said in muffled tones against his shoulder.

"When you disappeared, my heart struggled to beat. Now that I have you, it's beating again." He took her hand and placed it over his heart. "Do you feel that? It's my heart beating for you."

"I do," she said. She wrapped her hands around his neck, twinning her fingers through the hair at his nape, unwilling to let him go.

"I was hoping you would do me the honor of becoming my countess. Will you make me the happiest of men and marry me?"

She nodded. "I will."

Alan pulled her close and lightly grazed her lips before gently coaxing them open with his tongue. It took little persuasion.

She opened her lips and his tongue swept in and met hers, both swirling together in an entangled ritual of provocation and enticement. Her tongue pressed past his lips in a mutual give and take. The moment felt heady and hypnotic.

When he finally broke the kiss, he gazed into her eyes. "What about marrying on your birthday, my sweet?"

"That's very close. I like that idea," she said.

# EPILOGUE

## THE DAY AFTER THEIR WEDDING

*E*lizabeth rolled over and watched her husband, still asleep in their marriage bed. She could hardly believe the turn her life had taken since meeting this man. She still had to pinch herself to believe it was real. This handsome, wonderful man had made her his wife, and their wedding had been magical.

She and Alan were married by Special License in Hyde Park, next to the spot where his father used to take him to fish. The day Alan introduced her to that spot was the day she realized she was falling in love with him. They had taken their vows beneath the tree, with the clear, blue sky and the pristine water of the Serpentine providing the backdrop. When the vicar pronounced them married, snow had fallen. It had been a magical day for her. The day had been perfect.

Her mother-in-law and Madame Trousseau had insisted on a beautiful gown of rose-pink silk with a silver Alencon lace overlay and small seed pearls. Her russet-brown hair had been pulled back in a loose chignon with wispy curls escaping along the side and framing her face. Diamond pins were woven throughout the curls, and shoes made of white satin with seed pearls adorned her feet. A bouquet of greenery, red berries, and white roses with sprigs of lavender grass complemented her ensemble.

As he stirred, she ran her finger down his chest, loving the feel of his skin beneath hers.

"Good morning, wife," he said, pulling her close to him. "What are you thinking about?"

"All that has gone on in my life since meeting you. My stepbrother is being held for the crimes he committed and is suspected of causing the carriage accident that killed your uncle."

"I believe he thought getting rid of my uncle would get him closer to his stepfather's money. Only that didn't happen. I inherited Uncle Edward's responsibilities. The threatening letters I received will help prove their case. Yes, the man is bad news. His abduction of you was a bridge too far. At least he didn't hurt you," Alan said.

"No, he didn't. He would have if you had not found us," she said.

"I don't like to think of how close I came to losing you, darling. Luckily, Robbie, Trina, and Ross saved Jane, and she was able to tell us where you had gone," he said.

"Ha! That little boy and that dog are quite the pair. Did the doctor say how his mother is doing?" she asked.

"Not well. He doesn't expect her to live," Alan said softly.

"Oh, no! What will happen to him? He cannot live where he is."

"No . . . and we don't want him on the streets of East End. What would you think if we brought him to live with us?" Alan asked. "We cannot save his mother, but we can save Robbie."

She laid her head on his shoulder. "You are the most generous man I know. Robbie would love that."

"Speaking of Robbie, he helped Mother deliver all the boxing baskets—including his own," he said. "Trina was a big hit with the tenants. We had several requests for puppies—if she ever has them."

A knock sounded at the door.

"That would be our breakfast, my darling. My appetite is ravenous," he said, winking at her. "Are you hungry, my beautiful wife?"

"I am, handsome husband, but I think I need sustenance before I try more of the wonders you treated me to last evening," she said, smiling. The passion they had created had been wonderful, but she loved this time when they could talk, just the two of them.

"Put on your robe," he said, handing it to her as he got up from the bed and covered himself with his own. He went to the door.

"I finally found it, brother," Jeremy whispered, smiling in his sister-in-law's direction. Stepping back, a footman pushed a silver cart in and put the food on a small table that had been set up for breakfast. The footman lit a candle in the center of the table and left.

"Thank you, Jeremy. I mean it," Alan said, patting his brother's shoulder before he turned and left.

"Shall we break our fast, wife?" he asked temptingly.

Elizabeth came and sat next to him. "This is so beautiful."

"Why don't you dish up?" Alan said.

She lifted the silver dome covering a silver plate. Beneath it was a black box wrapped in velvet. Slowly, she opened the box, maintaining her gaze on her husband's smile.

"It's the locket my mother wore," she exclaimed, picking it up and hugging it to her heart. She opened it up to a miniature of her mother and father's painted portrait, the one her mother had worn every day of her married life. "Where did you find this?" she asked, wiping away tears.

"Mother told me what happened to it, and Jeremy found it for me," Alan said. "There's more." He nodded at the box.

She dug through the paper and found a sapphire and diamond ring. "My mother's ring," she said, crying. "I thought I'd never see this again in my lifetime."

Getting up from her chair, she pushed her way onto his lap and pulled his face to hers.

"I love you, my darling husband," she said. "I am starving, and I don't think eggs and rashers will fill me up."

"Can you give me a hint of what you want, dearest wife?" Alan teased.

"Yes . . . and it starts with those toe-curling kisses of yours," she said, covering his lips with hers.

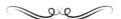

I hope you enjoyed
*EARL OF HALSBURG*
Make Mine An Earl Series
Book 4

**Please consider leaving a review
and/or rating on Amazon.**

All the best,
Anna St. Claire


P. S. Keep reading for a FREE PREVIEW of
*EARL OF WESTON*
Make Mine An Earl Series, Book 1.

# FREE PREVIEW

## EARL OF WESTON ~ MAKE MINE AN EARL SERIES ~ BOOK 1

LONDON, 1816

Edward Hunter, Earl of Weston, leaned back in his chair and stretched, having shaken hands with his opponent, the Earl of Harrington. He was looking for relaxation, and feeling only slightly buoyed by his win.

Edward was one monkey richer after five games of piquet and feeling strangely discomfited. His friend wanted to play on, but he promised he could recoup his losses another time. Around the elegant gaming saloon at the private gentlemen's establishment known as The Wicked Earls' Club, various games of chance were in progress: roulette, vingt-et-un, faro, whist, and hazard. At the far end of the room, the billiards table sent a series of loud 'click clack' noises echoing now and then, above the general hum.

Edward fingered the small gold 'W' insignia on the pin anchoring his neckcloth. It was a modest emblem, but every member was required to wear his when in attendance. He had been presented with the pin eight months ago, following his induction into the club.

While the club was not in the most fashionable district, it compared favorably with White's on the richness of its interiors. The walls were papered in either deep burgundy or hunter green tones throughout, and the lighting was low. Only the most masculine furniture—rich leathers, dark wood grains—appointed the club's public rooms.

This was no genteel hell. Whilst exclusive, The Wicked Earls' Club was a disreputable establishment. Edward allowed his gaze to travel over the heads of the other earls present. Some were doing their best to run through their fortunes before the year was out; others were living outrageously on the expectancy to inherit. In varying stages of disarray, these sons of gentlemen were lounging in the plush leather armchairs, swilling expensive wine as though it was ale, and engaging in good-humored ribaldry.

The lamps were turned low, apart from those above the tables, but from his discreet corner, Edward could see the flushed faces and smell the aromas of excitement and stale cologne. Beside the grand fireplace, one gentleman was playing hazard with the Earl of St. Seville, who had a large pile of promissory notes in his right hand. The man's hair clung in damp fronds to his brow and his cheeks burned a florid tale. He was clearly being fleeced. It was not an uncommon occurrence, but for some reason, Edward felt queasy and looked away. When had he become so easily affronted?

A blue haze of smoke wafted above the dark wood tables. Frederick, the Earl of Davenport, tilted his head back at that moment and added another long plume to the fog. Bright red splotches rode his cheekbones and his eyes held a wild expression that tobacco alone could not produce.

"Harrington," he called, as that earl approached the roulette table. "Care to try your luck against the bank?"

"Who holds the bank?" Harrington asked.

"I do."

"Then I must respectfully decline. You have the devil's own luck, Davenport."

Edward grinned. At least one of them was capable of exercising circumspection. Rising from his chair, he walked towards the door. An ear-splitting yelp, followed by booming laughter, caught his attention and he glanced back. Harrington had joined a lively game of hazard with the Earl of Grayson and some others. They appeared to be consoling Grayson on his losses in the time-honoured manner—with ridicule and banter. Unrepentant, Edward smiled and left the room to head down the hall in the direction of the morning room. Distracted by his thoughts, he opened the door in front of him. Too late, he realized he had intruded upon a private party.

"Weston! Join us."

He started at hearing his name, and peered into a low-lit, smoke-filled room, unable to make out the identity of the gentleman who had called out to him.

"Come on in, Weston. We have an extra." Edward knew he should recognize the sandy-headed man who had just pulled back from his pipe, but he could not place him. The man pointed to a meagerly clothed, dark-haired woman. She smiled and invited him to join her, beckoning with her finger.

"Thank you, but no." Edward gave an ironic bow. "If you will excuse me, I have a friend meeting me shortly." He backed out of the room, closing the door behind him. Spotting the door he was looking for, he opened it and fairly flew down the stairs to the first floor. The whole scene upstairs struck him as distasteful, and the sudden realization confused him.

A footman appeared with a salver bearing a selection of decanters and glasses and held open a door at the front end of the hall. Edward acknowledged the gesture. "You have perfect timing. Thank you."

"Yes, my lord." The servant's eyelids flickered but he gave no other sign of anything being untoward. Edward became conscious that a cloud of smoke had followed him and allowed the man a rueful nod. He sniffed his coat jacket and smirked. His valet would likely burn it. This jacket had been a favorite; it was comfortable. But there were plenty of others to replace it.

"I will have a brandy if there is still some to be had," he said, dismissing the footman to attend to his request. He entered the morning room and discovered it was empty. A smell of rich cherry tobacco greeted him. The corner fireplace had a small fire burning in the grate and warmed the room. The space was welcoming and would provide a pleasant respite from his earlier activity.

Edward hated his current circumstances. Having returned from Paris and his latest commission for the Crown, he had been met with devastating news. His brother was dead from a bullet discharged during a duel, but not a bullet fired by either duelist. And then, his father had died within a fortnight of Edward's return. He had no aspirations to take his father's title; it was supposed to have passed to his brother. Yet now he had inherited the earldom. Earl of Weston was not a role he had been trained to handle. It had been thrust upon him. His life now was damnable. He had responsibilities he had neither wanted nor sought, and the occupation he loved—working for the Crown—had been pushed aside. He missed his brother, Robert, and wondered how things had deteriorated so much between them. They had been close most of their lives. He was slowly accepting his responsibility for the arguments over his recklessness and gambling, realizing that they created many of their problems. *This should have been Robert's club.*

Leaning back, he propped his legs on an ottoman, comfortable in the brown leather chair tucked in the corner of the room. The Club had become his refuge, and he could now understand the other gentlemen's attachment to it. After an afternoon of gambling, he was content to nurse another brandy, thankful for the darkness and the quiet the club offered in which to scan the news sheets. Edward scrutinized the date—even last week's issue would be better than none, since he had not read it yet. It was late, so most of the members had left for evening assignations, excepting the few who were still occupied in the private rooms. He opened the paper and shook out the folds, hoping to read it without interruption. A salacious story sometimes succeeded in removing his thoughts from the pernicious life he was leading.

After a few minutes, he recognized the booming voice of his best friend, Thomas Bergen, greeting Henry, the club doorman in the entrance hall. Moments later, Bergen sauntered through the doors.

"Care for some company?" Not waiting for an answer, Bergen sat down and waved over a footman. "I think I shall catch up with you, old friend." He nodded towards the glass in Edward's hand. "I have had an especially profitable time at the tables, and am in the mood to relax."

"Of course. How fortuitous! It seems that Lady Fortune was smiling at both of us this day. I picked up a monkey—playing piquet, no less." Edward recalled the vowels he carried in his pocket. *If only I could have quit when I was ahead before now, perhaps Robert would still be alive.* His pain was profound.

Edward looked into his friend's face. The man was every bit his equal, and lately, his opposite. His dark eyes were usually full of laughter and promised levity. Edward, however, had rarely been in the mood for humor these past months. His mother used to remark on the two—Bergen's and his own dark hair, both heads of the same height. They were easy to spot. Women found Bergen hard to ignore. Maybe that was the reason for his constant smiling state; or, Edward reflected, it could be his friend's affable nature, which attracted the women. No matter; as far as he was concerned, Bergen and his good disposition were not welcome—at least today.

"Of course. Do as you please." Edward casually pulled out his cigarro case and slid it across the table to Bergen. "Have one." He did not really want company, but it was rare when Thomas, the fifth Earl of Bergen, did not also appear at the Club at the same time Edward was there. They had been friends since childhood, and he'd been the one to give his friend the nickname of Thomas which had stuck all these years. Bergen was more of a brother to him than his brother had been. He wondered why Robert kept invading his thoughts. A familiar sadness took root, and his attitude soured. *Fool that he was, he could not go an hour without thinking of his brother. Robert was there, a shadowy presence in every waking and sleeping moment.*

"What brings you here tonight, Bergen? As you might surmise

from my being in this corner, I was looking for a little time alone." Edward's tone was brusque but he knew Thomas was given to ignoring his temper, normally responding to it with humor.

"I must be impervious to that black mood of yours, because I still enjoy your company. Perhaps a jug of vinegar would help your temperament more than the expensive brandy you are quaffing." Bergen chuckled while swirling brandy in his glass. "Has there been any word on Hampton? I thought I had heard he was back in Town."

"No, none." Edward felt the hair on the back of his neck prickle, and he sat forward in the chair. "Where did you get your information? I find it odd that I was not also told. I left word with Colonel Whitmore, at Headquarters, to let me know as soon as he was sighted. He assured me they would let me know."

"I heard his name mentioned at a gaming hell, earlier tonight. It is quite curious. How long has it been, Edward?" Bergen lowered his voice and studied his friend.

"It has been nine months, and I am no closer to an answer." Edward finished his drink and poured himself another.

"I stopped at Headquarters on my way here. They may have news for you. The murder of a peer is serious business." Bergen rolled the unlit cigarro between his lips. "Have you received any more details?"

"No, nothing as yet. I am still hoping Hampton can provide a clue; maybe he saw something. Perhaps there is a connection to his prolonged disappearance." Edward stared into his brandy. Guilt at not being here for his brother seeped into his head, and he fought to keep his thoughts to himself. It was useless with Bergen.

"I know you feel some responsibility for Robert's death. Edward, you know it is nonsense. You were not in Town. You had no way to know what would happen. You were not here to stop the duel. And if you had been here, who can say there would have been a different outcome?"

"Logical and perceptive as always, Thomas." His tone was sarcastic. "The reasonable part of me knows that, but my heart will not accept it. Had I been here, I would have been Robert's second—providing I could not talk him out of such a foolish start."

"Believe it or not, I understand." Bergen's voice was compassionate.

The door from the back hallway flew open, hitting the wall with a crash. Several men, most likely emerging from the private rooms, were probably heading for new pursuits. Gaudily dressed women hung on the gentlemen's arms, displaying their wares with abandon. One woman wore a low-cut lace dress that barely covered her bosom; the other wore a bright yellow gown with black trimming which appeared to belong to someone a size or two smaller. Bright red lipstick and spots of heavy rouge drew attention to artificial faces. Perfumes of floral and fruit scents battled for distinction. Two more such women trailed behind the men, without partners. These were not the type of lady of whom his mother would approve.

One of the jades looked his way, and Edward realized too late that his brief glance had given her the wrong idea.

"My lord." A buxom blonde, with startling, bright red lips, tottered his way and sat on his lap. She was definitely not from his mother's circle, he thought, grinning.

"See something to amuse you, do you, handsome?" She boldly touched his face and allowed the tip of her tongue to peep between her teeth.

Edward felt her fingers slowly drifting across his cheek, coming to rest on his lips. Her seductive message was hard to mistake, particularly when she rocked her hips in a movement as old as time.

Bergen smirked and raised his glass. "Shall I give you some privacy?"

"No!" His voice elevated, Edward shot his friend a quelling glare. "That will not be necessary."

"What do you say I work the knots out of your shoulders, my lord?" She placed her hands on either side of his neck and rubbed deeply with her thumbs. "Hmm...is that pleasing to you, my lord?"

The woman winked at him, and smiled, showing red lip pomade carelessly smeared on her front teeth. She had obviously been employing her charms in one of the private backrooms. The thought repulsed him. "Madame, while I kindly appreciate your generous offer, I am not in the mood for any…entertainment." He moved her off his lap, and abruptly stood her on her feet. Digging into his pocket, he grabbed a gold coin and tossed it her way. "My friend and I were having a private discussion." He scowled, no longer amused. He had no interest in what she had to sell.

Miffed, she snatched up the coin and left, brushing off her red skirt as she rushed past him. Holding the handle of the door, she looked back.

"You could have used a good tumble, my lord," she said, her tone acetic. A moment later, he heard Henry call for the footman to usher them to the back door. His voice was a little more forceful than his usual tone. He had been surprised they were allowed in the morning room, and was glad to hear Henry send them out the backdoor.

Bergen whistled. "Losing your touch, are you, Edward? Making the ladies angry is not going to ease your needs." He sipped his drink and smiled.

"Have you anything important to tell me? If not, I have readied her for you." He rustled his paper, hoping his friend would take it as a sign he wanted to be alone.

Bergen chuckled. "Yes, as a matter of fact, I do have business with you. You know you cannot be rid of me so easily, Weston."

"I am all astonishment!" He did not really want his friend to leave and was glad he could not chase him off. "Damn! I am in worse shape than I thought. She did nothing for me." He looked at his lap, now disgusted with himself. "Maybe her amusement would have been just the thing." His body, however, told him otherwise.

"Along with the pox?" Bergen laughed, and then abruptly cleared his throat. "On a more serious note, I have a note for you." Reaching into his pocket, he pulled out a sealed letter and handed it to Edward.

"Coventry asked me to pass it on to you while I was at Head-quarters."

*Weston,*

*Hampton in town, and has been invited to the Bentley house party starting*

*on Friday. Has an interest in Lady Pennywaite. Invitations for you and Bergen are waiting at your homes. The visit could prove useful to your search. Acceptance already sent on both your and Bergen's behalf. Make plans to attend.*
*Coventry*

Edward wadded the note up and tossed it into the fire. "It seems I am going to a house party, my friend. I do not know the size of the affair, but it appears I need to go."

"It would appear we are both going. The man knows everything." Bergen grinned again. "Surely there will be card games, wagers, and ladies? This is the type of work I always enjoy. I suppose the invitations will give details of the location, but I believe the Bentley family is at their country estate. I will ride over in the morning and we can leave together, my friend."

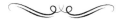

"Are you ready, Miss Longbottom?" the curate asked when he arrived to drive Hattie to the posting house to catch the stage.

"Bottom! Bottom!" Archie mimicked proudly. The curate's cheeks at once turned red.

"I suppose I am as ready as I can be," Hattie replied miserably, barely noticing her parrot's effrontery in the midst of her own distress.

"Little Whitley Parish will miss having you here," he replied while lifting her trunk and warily eyeing the large, exotic, green bird.

"I have never known anywhere else, but it was bound to happen sooner or later. Mrs. Bromley will take care of the flowers for the church, and will organize the sewing for the parish poor. Miss Gates will play the organ," she prattled on as they stood in the empty entrance hall.

"Your loss will be felt acutely," he said kindly. "For many years your family has been selfless servants to our parish."

"No one will know I am gone, before long," she said, dabbing at her eyes and blowing her nose with her handkerchief.

She pushed her spectacles farther up her nose and looked around. The house was empty and, she reflected with a pang of sadness, ready for the next occupants. It had not been a bad life, precisely, but very, very dull. Dull suited her admirably.

"I suppose there is no use in putting it off any longer. Come, Archie." Hattie held open the cage and the parrot obediently flew inside. She closed the front door behind her for the last time and walked out to the pony cart, feeling as though she was facing her doom.

The curate signaled the chestnut mare to move forward and she held onto Archie's cage with one hand and her bonnet with the other, as the cart lurched forward.

Harriet Eleanor Longbottom was a spinster. There was no other way to describe herself. She had given up her bloom to be a companion to her ailing mother, who by sly hints or subtle looks had convinced Hattie that she was indispensable to her health. Look at where it had left her, Hattie thought morosely. Somehow, six and twenty years had passed and not once had she left Worcestershire.

She had been faced with two choices when her mother died, and was grateful to have been permitted any opinion on the matter, for many were not so fortunate. She could live with her aunt, who had forbidden her to bring her beloved companion, Archie, or remove to Oxfordshire to her brother's estate and play aunt to his brood of five. There was really no choice.

Now, as she sat on the stage, crowded between two very large and disagreeable men, she was having second thoughts. One was a lecher, Hattie was convinced, for he sat as close as possible and was touching her leg on purpose! The other had never seen a bar of soap, she was certain, and her sense of smell would surely never be the same again.

It had been a very close thing to even be allowed on the stage with Archie. She had been obliged to pay an exorbitant bribe to the driver and still she had to hold the cage in her lap!

Across from her, a female of loose morals was displaying, in addition to heavily rouged cheeks, an overabundance of bosom overflowing from her scandalously low-cut scarlet gown. Hattie could not even look her in the eye, she was so ashamed as the woman flirted and exposed her ankles to the lecher.

The driver was moving at a frightful pace, and the conveyance tipped sideways around every bend in the road. Hattie prayed for all of their souls as steadfastly as she could, or sang hymns to Archie when he grew loud. He did have an unfortunate tendency to repeat words he heard or shriek when he was excited. She had never before considered she might be forced to travel on the stage with him.

When they stopped in Wolverstone for a change of horses, Hattie was most grateful for a chance to stretch her legs and breathe the fresh air. As she alighted precariously, her legs stiff, while at the same time balancing Archie's cage on her hip, a pair of riders flew by them, splashing mud all over the passengers and causing Hattie nearly to drop her bird.

Strings of oaths and curses were bellowed at the riders by driver and passenger alike, many of them words Hattie's pure ears had never before heard.

"Shite! Jackass!" Archie mimicked to roars of laughter. The sounds echoed around them.

"Mind your tongue!" she scolded Archie in horror, shaking her head as she did so. Her spectacles flew off and she heard the ominous sound of glass crushing.

"Drat!" she muttered, and fell to her knees to search for her faculty of sight. She was quite blind beyond five feet without them.

While the other passengers hurried inside to take advantage of the chance to refresh themselves, Hattie continued to search on the ground.

"Are you looking for these?" a deep, aristocratic voice asked. Dimly, Hattie perceived what remained of her spectacles as he held them out to her.

Something about the man's voice gave her pause and she did not want to look up at him. He was close enough that she could see his gleaming Hessians, and knew he was Quality. Suddenly self-conscious, she wanted to tidy herself before she stood up, but his hand was reaching down to assist her. His hands were large and elegant, even in his leather riding gloves, and they were strong enough to lift her lightly to her feet without apparent effort.

"Thank you, sir," she said with a slight tremble in her voice, still too shy to make eye contact, though she could make out most of his features from under her lashes.

The tall, dark stranger inclined his head and walked into the inn with his companion who had waited nearby, watching.

Hattie squinted after them, yet could see nothing but blurry movement.

Suddenly, she felt a pinch to her bottom and squealed in outrage. She turned to see the lascivious passenger; he was evidently amused by his antics as his large belly rumbled and his multiple chins quivered with laughter.

"How dare you!" she screeched with indignation.

"How dare you! How dare you!" Archie mimicked.

The driver blew the warning horn. She had not even managed five feet past the coach. How could it already be time to leave again?

"Driver!" She raised her voice, trying to get to his attention. "This man assaulted me and I refuse to ride inside with him!"

"She must be mistaken," the man said, feigning innocence. "Why would I want to touch her?" He sneered.

"Sorry, miss. Are there any witnesses?" the driver asked impatiently.

The other passengers shook their heads.

"Then we must be going. 'Tis your word against his."

Hattie watched as everyone climbed into the coach.

"I refuse to ride with this man. Sir, I must insist!"

"As you wish, miss." The guard slammed the coach door shut and hopped on the back as the driver gathered up the reins with a flick of the whip. The horses took off, splattering mud in her face. Spitting the excess earth from her mouth, she stared after the vehicle in disbelief, the distance growing rapidly as it sped away from her. What had just happened? Was there no goodness left in this world outside Little Whitley?

Hattie stood there for a full five minutes before she realized the implications of what had happened. She was stranded in a strange town without her belongings, except for a bird and her reticule.

Turning to face the inn, she picked up the cage and went inside.

The shabby inn was bustling with custom on this busy coaching road. Never before had she seen so many strangers. It smelled of smoke, sweat, and ale. She swallowed hard so she would not give in to her anger or her fright. Clearing her throat, she addressed the man she hoped to be the innkeeper since he seemed to be giving directions to the serving maids. It was her first time in such an establishment, and she had little idea how to proceed.

"Sir, could you please tell me when the next stage is due? The one I arrived on has left without me."

"Not until tomorrow, the same time," he grunted, looking at her with disapproval. She glanced down at herself; she had some splatters of mud, but certainly not outrageous in her blacks. Then she realized it was Archie he was staring at, an expression of considerable wariness shaping his features.

"What is your destination, miss?"

"I was to take this stage to Eynsham and my brother is to meet me there."

"It is only another few miles. Do you ride? I have horses for hire."

"I am afraid not," she replied.

"The gentlemen in the parlor are heading west, I think I heard them say."

"We are not acquainted," she said, bristling with affront. As if a single lady could ask a gentleman she did not know for anything, she wanted to point out.

"They have probably ridden here, anyway. You could walk," he suggested, clearly running out of patience.

She stared at the man in horror. She had spent six hours traveling in the most uncomfortable conditions, had been assaulted, and now her worldly possessions were lost.

"I must attend to the other customers. You may use the parlor, there are only the two gentlemen in there. He pointed to a door across the common room before he walked away. She watched him go, flustered and frustrated that she had no one to help her.

Hattie made her way as best she could through the blur to where she thought the parlor was. When she entered, she could not believe her eyes. Was she imagining things? She squinted.

No, there was indeed a barmaid sitting atop the knees of one of the gentlemen—and her chest was falling out of her bodice.

"I have walked into the devil's lair!" Hattie shrieked. Imagining the worst, she covered her eyes. She could see enough to know it was the gentleman and his friend from earlier, as the only thing she dared look at was his boots.

"Bugger, she's crazed." The second man laughed as the barmaid tried to tidy herself.

"Bugger! Bugger! Bugger!" Archie crowed unhelpfully, sensing his mistress's distress.

"Madam, cease your vapors at once!" one of the men commanded. "It is not at all what you think."

"I do not want to know, you imp of Satan! I know all about gentlemen such as yourself—whoremongers and, and rogues! Reverend Hastings reminds me every Sunday." She struggled to think of harsh enough names to call them.

"I am certain he does," the man said dryly.

Hattie's cheeks began to heat as she noticed the man looking her over like a piece of beefsteak. He was entirely too close for her comfort. Oh, no, he would not find her willing as the serving wench. She took Archie and ran for the door as fast as her feet would go. Five miles suddenly did not seem so far to walk.

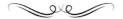

I hope you enjoyed this FREE PREVIEW of

*EARL OF WESTON*
Make Mine An Earl Series, Book 1

Tempted to read more?
**You can find it on Amazon.**

Happy Reading,
Anna St. Claire

# HEART TO HEART

Dear Reader:
You are cordially invited to join my Heart to Heart Community.

Get the inside scoop on upcoming releases including the next Make Mine An Earl book.

Plus sneak peeks, freebies, contests and more.

No spammy stuff.
Only yummy stuff.

**Join:**
**Anna St. Claire's Heart to Heart Newsletter**
**And get a *Noble Hearts Series Free Preview*!**

**Or you can visit my website:**
**annastclaire.com**

Happy Reading,
Anna St. Claire

# ABOUT THE AUTHOR

*Who knew I'd become an author?* Not me. But when the opportunity came, I grabbed it and approached it like I've done everything in my life—celebrating the hits and laughing at the misses. Nothing worthwhile is easy, and that includes everything in my life. But I have much to smile about—a beautiful daughter, two precious granddaughters, my adorable dogs, and my sweet husband of over thirty years. He has always supported me—including uprooting to move to the other side of Charlotte, N.C. for a life change, just when we thought we were *settled*.

If *settled* means nothing changes, then it'll never describe me. I give everything to things I enjoy—and that includes writing. In 2021, I hit the **USA Bestselling Author** list, and recently, two of my favorite books were named ***RONE* Finalists**!

My daughter avoids crowded movies with me because I'm *that woman* in the row in front of you who gleefully munches her popcorn and laughs at every hilarious scene. Loudly. Besides my family, I love chocolate, popcorn, laughter, and animals. To keep memories of my pets alive, I frequently sprinkle them in my stories as secondary characters. British and American history has always interested me, so writing historical romances in those genres always excites me.

When I was barely three, my mother moved my sister and me from New York to the Carolinas. Juggling a full-time job and full-time school, my mother became my first genuine hero—never waving the flag when things were tough. Things quickly got tough. My grandmother, who taught me to read before I started first grade, died before I was seven and I've never forgotten her.

Margaret Mitchell's *Gone with The Wind* remains one of my favorite stories, but Kathleen Woodiwiss' books, Shanna, and Ashes in The Wind, hooked me on historical romance and the dream of writing.

While I primarily write Regency romance, I enjoy almost any period in American and British history.

Connect with me via my website: www.annastclaire.com
Email: annastclaireauthor@gmail.com
Or on social media.

## MAKE MINE AN EARL SERIES

### EARL OF WESTON
BOOK 1

### EARL OF BERGEN
BOOK 2

### EARL OF SHEFFORD
BOOK 3

### EARL OF HALSBURG
BOOK 4

## NOBLE HEARTS SERIES

### THE EARL SHE LEFT BEHIND
BOOK 1

### ROMANCING A WALLFLOWER
BOOK 2

### THE DUKE'S GOLDEN RINGS
BOOK 3

### MY LORD, MY ROGUE
BOOK 4

### SILVER BELLS AND MISTLETOE

BOOK 5

<u>SCANDAL BENEATH THE STARS</u>

BOOK 6

<u>NOBLE HEARTS BOX SET</u>

**EMBATTLED HEARTS SERIES**

<u>EMBERS OF ANGER</u>

BOOK 1

**OTHER TITLES**

<u>A WIDOW'S PERFECT ROGUE</u>

<u>ODDS ON AN EARL</u>

<u>THE DUKE'S GOLDEN BELLE</u>

Printed in Great Britain
by Amazon

35701484R00078